PIG
PAUL GERAGHTY

"My name's Michael Goodenough. I live in Riverside Road, near the soccer club, and I have a sister in Class Two . . . I mean, Sub B. We call it Class Two in Greytown."

"Tell us about Greytown," interrupted Mr Stirling.

"Greytown is a small town surrounded by farms and plantations. Um, the main thing they farm, or I s'pose they aren't actually farms . . ." (I could see my marks flying out the window) "is trees. Wattles and pines and um . . . and . . . well mainly wattles and pines. We had a pig farm. And my best friend was Phocho . . ." (I wondered what Phocho would have thought if he'd known how famous I was making him.) ". . . Um, he's a Zulu, and he lives on the compound near the farm."

I heard a few hisses of muted laughter, as if it was a big joke or something. Mr Stirling stopped watching me for a moment to glare dangerously at the class, then he looked back and nodded for me to continue.

"We had the second-biggest private pig farm in Natal . . ."

RED

A Red Fox Book

Published by Random House Children's Books
20 Vauxhall Bridge Road, London SW1V 2SA

A division of Random House UK Ltd

London Melbourne Sydney Auckland
Johannesburg and agencies throughout
the world

First published in 1988 by Maskew Miller Longman,
Cape Town.
First published in Great Britain in 1991
by Hutchinson Children's Books

Red Fox edition 1992

3 5 7 9 10 8 6 4 2

Copyright © Paul Geraghty 1988

Printed and bound in Great Britain by
Cox & Wyman Ltd, Reading, Berkshire

RANDOM HOUSE UK Limited Reg. No. 954009

Papers used by Random House UK Limited
are natural, recyclable products made from wood grown in
sustainable forests. The manufacturing processes conform to
the environmental regulations of the country of origin

ISBN 0 09 989710 5

Dedication

**For my class of '84
at Aliwal Road,
who always welcomed
a new face.**

Dear Olivia

Hope you enjoy pig's tale!

Paul Geraghty

Contents

Chapter 1

Stinking bogeyheads

Jenny was really proud of her new uniform.

To tell you the truth, mine made me feel a bit scared. Somehow I wasn't ready to meet new people. I just had a kind of a gut-feeling that they'd be a bunch of chops one way or another, but there was no turning back. We were headed on a mission into the unknown. Bombing targets at a new school.

The school that Uncle Ray had told Mom about was full, so we got booked into a much smaller, ancient little place just across the road from it.

I was glad in a way, because there wouldn't be quite so many big hackers to have to try and get on with. It also meant that Jenny and I would go to the same school because it was for boys and girls. You might think I would have preferred to have gone to a different school from my whining little lightie of a sister, but you're wrong. It's really pathetic, I know, but I was secretly glad that we could walk to school together. Of course I pretended it was feeble and all, but inside I was glad.

Jenny wasn't at all worried. She wouldn't shut her gob for a minute all the way up the road, past the soccer club, over the railway bridge (which I felt like jumping off . . . sort of) across the main road and into Chelsea Road, which was where the school was.

My heart was really going, as I saw more and more people in the same blue uniform heading towards the school. I checked them out as if they were already enemies, sort of trying to work out if I could beat them in a rumble if I had to, and this kept making my heart beat harder. And all the time, Jenny jabbered away. I was too scared to tell her to shut up in case my voice quivered and gave away how much I was nipping myself. It was pathetic. Really pathetic.

"I wonder if my new teacher will also like hamsters," Jenny said.

I couldn't believe it! I mean, how could she think about hamsters at a time like that?

"I'm going to be the best drawer in the whole class. I can draw horses better'n anybody . . ."

Someone checked me out. My hair prickled all over. I could tell he was looking at me because I was new, the way dogs sniff each other when they meet in the street. He stood at the gate like a main ou, with hair covering the tops of his ears, looking me up and down as if I was for sale or something. His friends hung around next to him, also checking me out. They'd all suddenly stopped talking when they saw me. Even a group of girls beyond them had stopped to stare. I looked back at him, but he stared straight at me, so I had to look away, and I walked past him facing the other way, hoping he wouldn't say anything.

As I crossed the gateway he spoke, and my face went hot like it does when you've been caught doing something illegal.

"Are you the new ou?" he demanded.

I said, "Yeah," but my voice squeaked, so I sounded like a complete wally. From the corner of my eye I thought I saw him smile slightly, and as I walked away I could feel their eyes drilling into me. I couldn't walk normally because I knew I was being watched. My arms wouldn't swing properly and my bum cheeks were clamping together like a vice, but I had to keep on going without looking back.

What a childish question: "Are you the new ou?". I mean, what does he think — I'm some regular ou in disguise? One of them said something and they all burst out laughing. I knew they were laughing at me. Big joke. So my voice slipped. I could think of funnier things than that to laugh about. It looked as if I was right. This lot were going to be a bunch of stinking, pathetic bogeyheads, just like I'd expected.

I didn't know what to do with myself, so we walked through an archway into a closed-in place which I later found out was called the quad. People charged around, screaming, chasing and laughing all over the show. Each time new people noticed us, they'd shut up suddenly and behave all cool while checking us out. Jenny and I stumbled about like lost sheep in a lion's den. It wasn't so bad in the quad though, because all the lighties hung around there and I didn't really care so much if they stared. You can't blame lighties really.

All the main ous seemed to hang around at the gate with that big chop who obviously thought he owned the place.

I felt really spare walking around with my bag still in my hand, because everyone else had put theirs down outside different classrooms. No one told Jenny and me where to put ours. That made us stick out like sore thumbs even more.

There was a teacher wandering around by the tennis courts as we went out to the back of the school. A swarm of kids ran up to her and started yelling and pointing at us until she came over.

"Hello, are you the Goodenough children?"

There was a whole zoo of lighties standing behind her, watching us.

"Yes miss."

Some stupid girl said "Goodenough" and started giggling with her friend.

"We heard you were coming today. I'm Mrs Harvey. Have you met your teachers yet?"

"No."

"Oh well, follow me and I'll show you your classrooms and call your teachers from the staff-room for you."

She started walking towards the quad, then stopped and turned to us again. "You're in Standard Five, um . . . Mark, is it?"

"Michael, yes."

"And you're Jenny?"

3

"Yes." She was all bright and keyed-up.

Quite funny really, *she* was fine, while her big, tough brother was just about wetting himself.

"You will be with Miss Johnstone, Jenny. Come along and I'll call them for you."

She took off again, and all the lighties started chattering away like a gang of monkeys with their latest consignment of banana trees. She pointed out our classrooms on the way and we dumped our bags, which made me feel a bit more normal. Only slightly though, because people were still gawking at us. Then she took us down a corridor which must have been out of bounds because there were no rubber-neck kids hanging around, which made a change after being on show like that.

We waited outside the staff-room while Mrs Harvey called our teachers.

Mine was a really scary-looking bloke. A giant-sized man with hundreds of craters and bits of beard on his chin, called Mr Laing. Jenny's teacher looked quite nice. She was young and friendly. I secretly wished she was my teacher, and that I could be a lightie again. I know it was stupid, but that's what I felt like.

Mr Laing said that he had a spare desk and a set of books ready for me and that when the bell went I had to line up with the other Standard Fives at one end of the quad. Mrs Harvey took Jenny with her to meet some other Class Twos who'd show her where to line up when the bell went.

Suddenly I was on my own. I looked down the dark corridor towards the brightness in the quad. What the hell was I supposed to do? There wasn't anyone to talk to and I didn't want that slimy bogeyhead to see me again, but I couldn't stay in the corridor, because I knew it was out of bounds.

Just then the bell saved me from having to bother. I suppose that's what saved by the bell means. It was an electric one. Really larney. It just about made me jump out

4

of my skin that first time it went off, then I ran down the corridor to the quad and stood next to a pole on one side.

A whole lot of tiny kids started swarming around me, and then I realised I'd gone to the wrong side. As I headed towards the proper side, I noticed that the big docus who'd asked the stupid questions at the gate was looking at me. So were his mates. They were laughing again because I'd been waiting on the wrong side with the Class Ones. My face started going hot again like before, and I couldn't stop it.

When I got to the Standard Five line, I moved to the back and sort of hovered around where they couldn't see me without turning around. So what happened? Some weed in front of me turns round and reckons, "Why's your face so red?"

He looked right at me and I didn't know what to do, so I just said, "It's not," which was really stupid, because I could feel that it was, and anyway how could I tell when I couldn't see my own face?

He stared at me as if I was mad or something for a few really uncomfortable seconds, then shook his head and turned to face the front. I couldn't believe it. I felt as if they'd all planned to be as lousy as possible to me without even knowing what I was like.

The bell rang again, a long, raspy shot that ripped at my ears from the wall in the quad, and suddenly the talking stopped. My teacher with the craters came out and stood in front of everyone while the other teachers hung around on the side next to the Class Ones, near where I'd stood by mistake.

"That was the second bell," he shouted, "there's to be no talking after the second bell. And if you don't get my drift, we'll all have to practise keeping quiet after school, won't we?"

Everyone was dead quiet. A teacher coughed in the gap before Mr Laing carried on. "This afternoon's junior soccer practice has been cancelled."

A few of the lighties groaned. I immediately felt better. I'd forgotten about soccer. At least that was something to look forward to. Unless those wombats kept me out of their team.

The voice carried on. "So, junior soccer players, unless you want to watch the seniors, don't forget to make the necessary arrangements for getting home."

The weed turned round and whispered to me, "Do you play soccer?"

I was just about to answer when the voice up front thundered, "That's the last time I'm warning you! The next person who utters so much as a peep will be staying in detention this Friday!"

I don't know whether he heard the weed talking or whether he heard someone else, but the head in front of me shot round like a catapult and aimed forwards without moving.

Mr Laing sounded a bit dangerous. I decided then that I'd better not try any stirring with him. Actually, at that stage I was busy racking my brains for an excuse to get out of that school.

Another gumtree of a teacher told the girls something about a netball match, and then we led off to our classrooms.

I was in the biggest class in the school. There were thirty-five of us in Standard Five, including me. Twenty of them were girls, who mostly seemed pretty snotty types that wouldn't be bothered with having anything to do with the likes of me. Then there were fifteen blokes.

Mr Laing put me in a desk next to someone called Francis, who was supposed to help me out with anything I hadn't done at my old school in Greytown. I recognised him as one of the main ous who'd been standing at the gate when I arrived, but he didn't seem too bad on his own.

"So what's your name again then?" he asked, even though Mr Laing had just told the whole class who I was, and of course they all thought my surname was hilarious.

"Michael, or . . . Mike, actually."

"I'm Francis." It sounded like a girl's name to me, but I didn't say anything. I only discovered later that it was spelt different. "Drac's not too bad really, just as long as you do your work properly."

"What?" At first I thought he was talking about the heavy who stood at the gate.

"Mr Laing. We call him Dracula. He's not a bad bloke, we put up with him."

"Oh," I said, feeling a bit of a cabbage for not realising who he was talking about.

"He's not too strict, just as long as you get your work right. You're not thick are you?"

"Uh, no." I didn't know whether I was or not. Phocho was the only one I'd ever compared marks with at the farm school, and we used to do about the same, so I reckoned I couldn't be all that thick. Besides, I wasn't going to let them think I was thick, even if it turned out that I was.

We started off with a maths lesson, working with decimal fractions, which wasn't too bad. It was all stuff I'd done before, thank goodness, because I was feeling lousy enough as it was without having to discover that I was the thickest in the class as well. Especially after telling Francis that I wasn't.

I actually found a mistake in his work, which I pointed out to him. He said "Thanks," but I don't reckon he was too happy about it. So, apart from being stared at just about the whole time by one person or another, I managed to get through the morning without dying.

Then the dreaded break bell went.

It's absolutely pathetic being scared of break time. I mean, that's what makes school bearable, going out to break. But there I was wishing that breaks didn't exist. Desks opened and slammed and books flopped and flew as everyone scrambled things away and scrummaged for the door.

The main ou from the gate, whose name I discovered was Trevor, was rousing everyone up for a game of stingers. He yelled like a maniac, holding the fluorescent tennis ball above his head as if he was about to brand someone before they even got out of the classroom.

They all ran off to the tennis court and made a ring of players to see who would be *on*.

Some girls from our class sat on the wall outside the enclosure to watch, so I picked a spot a safe distance away and watched as well.

They stooped down and started butting the ball about with their fists until it went between someone's legs, then they ran like chickens in all directions as the bloke who was *on* picked the ball up. It was Francis. He chased Trevor halfway round the court, then threw as hard as he could. I quietly hoped it would really sting him. In fact, I wished the ball was made of lead, so that it would knock his block off. But it missed.

He tried again, and the ball flew harmlessly against the fence, spraying terrified people away from it wherever it rolled. On his third try, Francis branded Benjy, a big, slow bloke, and then they worked as a team, passing the ball back and forth, because once two people are *on*, they aren't allowed to run with the ball. Bunches of people screamed and fled each time the ball came near, and gradually more and more people were branded, but Trevor was still free.

After a few more minutes of chasing around, Trevor was the only one who hadn't been branded. The whole tennis court was against him, and I rubbed my hands together in glee. He ran like a wild thing between the players as they shouted and chased for the ball. Every time they tried to brand him, he skipped into the air and crumpled himself to avoid being hit. He timed each throw perfectly, fisting shots out of the way, then running in the opposite direction, leaving the others to collect the ball and build up another attack. Without even seeming to look, he would jump and dodge that steaming ball until I didn't believe it could go on any longer. One shot shaved against his rods, but he reckoned it missed. And then there was a bit of an argument. Gradually people started siding with him until everyone agreed that it was a miss.

Then, just as the chase was about to begin again, the bell went. Someone shouted, "Hey, he can't get away with this!"

which was greeted by a wall of cheers as they all piled in to hold him down and brand him.

"Pile on! Pile on!" they shouted. I felt like joining in.

But even in the face of those overwhelming odds he didn't give up. He kicked and thrashed around, twisting his hands free in a desperate attempt to escape. I stood up, ready to run to the quad, but with my head screwed on backwards to enjoy the moment I'd been waiting for all along.

In the fight his shirt had come untucked, so they twisted him round until his bare back faced Mally. He raised the ball above his head, then threw as hard as he could. The trouble was, he tried so hard that his aim was pretty shoddy, and the ball crashed onto Leon's wrist instead. He howled out in pain, and Trevor roared with laughter. So did everyone else as they turned and ran for the quad. I got to our spot just as the second bell went, but all the others were still running up from the tennis court.

"Right!" roared Mr Laing, "those Standard Five boys, I warned you this morning. You've been here long enough to know that you've got two minutes until the second bell. And being the seniors of the school doesn't mean you can choose to ignore the bell whenever you please."

"But sir, we were playing sting . . ."

"I don't care if you were rescuing the last dodo, when the bell goes, you *move*!"

There was a deathly hush as we waited for the sentence.

"Right, so the Standard Five boys can stay after school today and practise getting to their lines on time."

There were reluctant groans behind me, and I wondered what Mom would think of this lot, me getting kept in on my first day. Jenny would obviously tell her, even if I let her be a Lancaster bomber for the rest of the year. She wouldn't be able to resist a juicy story like that one.

Then Mr Laing carried on: "I make two exceptions. I notice that Mr Green and Mr Goodenough were good enough to get to our lines on time." Everyone laughed at the stale joke (I suppose it wasn't stale for them, but I was fairly sick

of people thinking they'd discovered it for the first time).
"So they can leave at two-thirty with the rest of the school."

A voice behind me hissed "Suction!", and the others started moaning under their breaths that I'd also been late.

"Surridge! What's your problem? Would you like to tell me about it?" Mr Laing looked as if he was about to lose his rag. Maybe that was why he was called Dracula.

"No sir."

"Right, then we'll see you here at two-thirty sharp. Any dawdling and you'll stay even longer. I don't care how much soccer practice you miss."

During the strained silence that followed I reminded myself to ask how to go about joining the soccer team.

"Lead off."

We had woodwork after break, and of course because I was the fifteenth chap, I had to work at a bench on my own while all the other blokes worked in pairs. Making friends with this gang of lenses was going to be even more difficult than I thought.

The woodwork teacher was an old dinosaur called Mr Wilkinson, with giant-size, whistling nostrils filled with bushes of white hair. He wore bullet-proof glasses that balanced down on the end of his nose like they do on grandmothers in fairy tales.

He told me that I had to bring money to pay for the measly piece of wood he gave me to start making a bookshelf. All the others had been working on their "models", as he called them, for about two weeks, and I had a bit of catching up to do, so he hung over me and helped me for most of the lesson, except when Hedley Bloumeyer cut his finger with a file.

The whole class was called round for a big lecture about not following simple instructions, while Hedley had to stand with his finger under the running tap and nearly got his head eaten off for trying to take it out too soon. Even though Mr Wilkinson had railway-tunnels for a nose, he had to breathe through his mouth a bit as well, so that there was this funny hissing and whistling noise right down my neck for just about the whole two periods. He really gave me the creeps.

When the sandpapering and filing eventually came to an end, we joined up with the girls, who'd been to needlework, for geography. Mr Laing gave me a whole pile of notes and asked Amanda Pierce to lend me her book to catch up all the stuff that they'd already done. Most of it was different from what Phocho and I did at the old farm school, so my heart started nervousness into me about whether I'd be able to handle the big city-type of schoolwork or not. I realise now how stupid I was to have worried, but I didn't know how easy it was going to be at the time.

While Mr Laing rattled on about Amsterdam and Rotterdam and fishing and things, I found myself thinking about stingers. Sometimes we used to play at the old school, and I was quite a keen player. I had an argument with myself about whether I should ask to play with them or wait till they invited me to join in. No one had even thought of asking me at little break, but then again they were already starting by the time I got to the tennis court. The first thing I'd do would be to brand Trevor a real steamer of a shot . . .

"*Goodenough!*"

I leapt out of my body. It was Mr Laing's voice.

"Sir?"

"Stand up when you speak to a teacher, boy, you're not in the wilderness any more."

I tried to runckle my desk loose from the chair, but they were hooked together, so I had to sort of stand up with my knees bent and the desk tilting dangerously forwards. "Sir?"

"Are you finding this lesson boring?"

"No sir."

"Well then kindly try and stay awake so that I know you're still with us."

There were a few chuckles around the class and I felt my face going hot again. I was having a bit of a disastrous day all round.

"Sit! Stay! And don't play dead this time."

11

There were more chuckles because he was talking to me like giving instructions to a dog. This Dracula chap was quite a card, or so he and the class thought.

I rattled my chair and desk apart roughly so that the class wouldn't think I was a naff, then sat down and tried to look normal. Some bloody idiot girl who looked like a hippo carried on staring at me until Mr Laing gave her a mouthful too, then I felt better.

I concentrated on concentrating for a while, but after a few minutes I was thinking about stingers again. Suddenly I noticed Mr Laing staring at me with daggers in his eyes. He had stopped talking, but carried on as soon as I tuned in again. I took a deep breath. That had been a close shave.

The bell rang and Francis just about dived over his desk for the door, but Mr Laing held us back till he'd finished before letting us go.

As I shut my desk, Trevor shouted, "It's open season!"

All the blokes cheered wildly and the girls screamed and scattered ahead of them, because obviously open season meant that they were going to cop it, as they say in the war comics. Within seconds the room was empty.

I went out to see what they were up to, and as I stepped into the sunlight, Trevor came belting past me with the ball in his hand, just about knocking me over. They chased each other round the dirty prefabs, making more hand marks on the corners, which showed how often they'd played the game before. The girls screamed every time Trevor came round the corner, but I could see that they actually really liked him. It made me feel pretty miserable. I mean, I didn't fancy girls all that much anyway, but it would have been nice to have someone on my side. Even girls. Some were okay, the ones that didn't scream and squeak too much. But if this lot thought Trevor was a hero, they couldn't have been up to much. They'd probably also take up laughing at me if my voice slipped or something.

I looked round to see who I could ask about the soccer team, but everyone was too busy to talk to me. They were all quite happy to look at me and talk to each other, but they weren't interested in talking to me. They must have thought I was really thick if they didn't know I knew. I could just tell that the whole place was filled with enemy people. There wasn't a single person half as nice as any of the decent blokes from the farm school. I mean, even the pathetic lighties at the farm school were better than these stinking bogeyheads.

There was one bloke in my class that I thought I might be able to get on with. He was the only other one apart from me who hadn't played stingers at little break. And about the only one who hadn't been laughing at me all day, one way or another. He was a small bloke with glasses, called Peter Green. He seemed a bit strange because he kept his blazer on even though it was so hot.

I noticed he was on his own again, leaning against the concrete fence next to the music room, playing a pocket-size Donkey Kong game. He was out of the way of the action, so I decided to go and talk to him.

As I approached him, I noticed hundreds of tiny white dots on his shoulders. His hair was greasy and black. I thought *I* was supposed to be quite a dirty type, but I could tell that his hair was in desperate need of a good wash.

When I tried to talk to him he didn't even look up. He just lifted his shoulder and turned away from me, his thumbs pushing like crazy at the plastic buttons, making the little black thing beep around the electric jungle.

I walked back down to the prefabs where the others were playing, hoping someone would ask me to join in, or at least talk to me. It was ridiculous. Fun was happening all over the show, and I stood in the middle of it as if I was poisonous or something.

A gang of screaming people charged past, and one girl grabbed onto my shoulder as she raced round the bend. I stumbled to keep my balance. Trevor ran past with the dreaded ball raised in his right hand. I was busy dusting myself off when he turned to me and got ready to brand me a hard shot. I crumpled to take cover, but he didn't throw.

Instead he laughed mockingly as if I was a coward, and raced off after the screaming girls.

I decided that the school really stank, and even sulked to myself that I wouldn't play soccer if it had to be with such lousy chops. I'd rather sit at home and do nothing than have to be in the same team as those lenses.

Break was so long. I just wished it would end.

By the time the bell went I thought I'd had enough for one lousy day, but I hadn't bargained for the double English with Mr Stirling that followed. He was our Principal, so everyone was on their best behaviour with him. He came into the classroom and immediately there was silence. Everybody stood up like mongooses and waited until he told us to sit down. After a long silence, during which he looked over the whole class as if he was trying to catch someone doing something wrong, he said, "Today we're going to do a comprehension." (Francis let out a very shy groan that only I could hear.) "But before we start, I'd like to get an oral mark for our new boy here." He pointed at me and my heart nearly leapt out of its mountings. I stood up quickly. "Michael Goodenough."

"Yes sir?" My voice was hardly more than a whisper. He frowned and I realised that I'd already done something wrong.

"You must speak up, boy. You're not a mouse are you?"

Nobody laughed.

"No sir."

"Good. Have you introduced yourself to the class yet?"

I swallowed at a rock in my throat. "No sir."

"Well, now's your chance. The class has just completed a set of impromptu talks, and I think it would be quite appropriate for you to tell us a little bit about yourself, don't you?"

The rock was unswallowable, and I could feel my voice wanting to squeak again. "Yes sir."

"Well, come out here then, and let's hear who you are and where you come from."

I didn't think my legs would carry me to the front of the class, but they made it.

"Well, come on then," he said impatiently.

I cleared my throat and began with a voice that didn't shiver quite as much as I'd feared it would. "My name's Michael Goodenough. I live in Riverside Road, near the soccer club, and I have a sister in Class Two . . . I mean, Sub B. We call it Class Two in Greytown."

"Tell us about Greytown," interrupted Mr Stirling.

"Greytown is a small town surrounded by farms and plantations. Um, the main thing they farm, or I s'pose they aren't actually farms . . ." (I could see my marks flying out the window) "is trees. Wattles and pines and um . . . and . . . well mainly wattles and pines. We had a pig farm. And my best friend was Phocho . . ." (I wondered what Phocho would have thought if he'd known how famous I was making him.) ". . . Um, he's a Zulu, and he lives on the compound near the farm."

I heard a few hisses of muted laughter, as if it was a big joke or something. Mr Stirling stopped watching me for a moment to glare dangerously at the class, then he looked back and nodded for me to continue.

"We had the second-biggest private pig farm in Natal . . ."

Before I knew it I was sliding back onto my chair and pulling myself up against the desk. It hadn't been as bad as I'd expected, but I could tell that the blokes were really excited about Phocho, or this pig farm business. At best I hoped that they might have been impressed by the size of the farm, but I suspected that they probably just thought living on a pig farm with a Zulu friend was a huge joke, just like my name and everything else about me.

That afternoon I walked home after one of the most rotten days of my life, pretending nothing was wrong. I had to hang back a bit at one point, because I started catching up with two girls from my class who were dawdling up ahead. One was the fat hippo of a female, whose name turned out to be Celia.

15

The other one was quite pretty, as girls go, and she was called Janine. I didn't want them to see me, but they kept walking slower and slower until they eventually stopped outside a block of flats, where one of them obviously lived. So I ducked into a side street before they could spot me, and took a sort of detour home. The only thing was, the roads didn't quite work out the way I'd expected, and I ended up getting totally lost.

At home, Jenny rattled on non-stop about all the kids in her class that she was already best friends with, and all that junk, and when Mom asked me how my day was, I just said it was okay.

She asked me if I'd found out about the soccer, and I felt so guilty about my decision not to play that I lied and said Francis was going to tell me, but he didn't have time and would tell me the next day. I knew it was a pretty flimsy excuse, but Jenny was so busy sprouting forth, and Mom was so wound up about starting her new job the next day, that they didn't even notice. They probably didn't even hear what I said, come to think of it.

I copied geography notes all evening, and that night I had a horrible dream about stingers.

Chapter 2

On Porcupine Hill

We'd had to leave the farm in Greytown because my dad died.

It was belting down with rain the day I heard. Sunday the twenty-fifth of March. I'd just made myself an eggnog and had the first sip when Mom came into the lounge from outside looking like a stranger, just staring at me. Staring like a ghost. Her hair strung down and her face was wet, but it wasn't from the rain. There was terrifying electricity in the air. Our eyes locked together in fright because we couldn't talk. Then she sniffed and just broke down. "It's Daddy," she'd said, like a little girl.

I'd poured the perfect eggnog down the sink and locked myself away, feeling totally alone and helpless.

Mom could never have run the farm on her own. It would have got pretty lonely out there without Dad, I can tell you. Even in a suburb full of people it was hard enough trying to get by on our own. Uncle Ray had found a job for Mom in Cape Town, so there we were, living in a box in Wynberg without a dad.

I remember what an idiot I felt putting on a suit for the funeral. How I could have worried about something so stupid I don't know. I looked just like all the old fossils, but it was my own dad and all, so I suppose it was the right thing to do. Even Phocho, my school connection, had to wear one, so it wasn't all that bad.

Actually, Phocho was more than just a school connection, he was the rest of my class. We were the only two in Standard Five, that's how small the school was. Quite pathetic, really.

There were only nineteen of us in all the years put together. And Phocho was the only Zulu. All the rest of us were white.

We lived right out in the sticks, too far from the main school, so we had to go to the stupid old farm school.

In the beginning there was a big stink about getting Phocho into the school. They said blacks weren't allowed, and a whole lot of other junk, but Dad told them off and wrote hundreds of letters and things and had huge fights with everyone about getting him in, until finally they had to say yes.

Then of course the Oliviers on the farm next door were so cheesed off about their stupid brats sitting in class with a Zulu that they took them out and sent them off to some Afrikaans boarding school, where they reckoned they would get a proper education. Good luck to them, I reckon. At least I had someone my own age to go to school with. And he was my best mate as well.

Jenny sat in the front row and told Mom whenever I caused trouble, which was a bit of a nuisance, but I suppose it helped me to pay attention and all that other boring stuff you have to do to keep the teacher happy.

I'd been trying to straighten my stupid tie when Phocho came into the room and immediately cracked up laughing at me in my larney clothes. He didn't seem to realise that he looked just as much of a chop in his suit. The only thing was, I didn't really feel like laughing just then. It had been a week since Dad had died. Only a week, but it had also been a long time. I was getting better at not crying, but the truth was I hadn't learned how to laugh again.

Mom had acted all brave in front of the aunts and uncles and things that came to Oakdale for the funeral. Some of them said we'd have to give up the farm and the pigs, and then others had huge arguments about how it would all be paid for by insurance because it was a hunting accident, but no one really knew at that stage. Not even us.

"I've never been to a *abelungu* funeral before," said Phocho. He'd stopped laughing, and spoke kindly because

18

he noticed I wasn't feeling all that hot. Like the good friend he really was.

"Nor've I."

"I wonder, do you have to kneel and things, like normal church?"

"I s'pose so."

He looked at me for a long time, then said, "You think you must leave the farm now?"

It had been on both of our minds all the time, but we hadn't had the guts to come out with it.

"I don't know. I hope not."

His eyes were soft, and he searched right inside me, into the back of my head as I spoke, to see if there was something there that I wasn't telling him.

"I don't know how we're gonna cope without Dad. He did everything." I sighed heavily. "Whatever happens, we'll stay somewhere round here, that's for sure."

Phocho's eyes lit up. "If your Mom can't keep the place, you can come and live with us! At the compound. Just think, we could go riding and shooting any day!"

"And we could have lubalala contests with Sipho," I chirped up, getting quite excited for a moment.

". . . And soccer matches!"

We'd known it could never happen that way. I couldn't see Mom living in a Zulu compound, and guns weren't allowed there either, but it was fun to think about Nyaga keeping us after Dad had kept him.

Nyaga was Phocho's father. He was also *Induna* on the farm and head of the compound. Dad reckoned he was a true Zulu in the old noble tradition or something. Sort of like Dingaan and Shaka, I suppose.

In the silence we heard Mom calling from the front door, and as we moved I said, "I hope we don't have to leave."

I'd known I wouldn't like the funeral. Everyone wore black and sniffed from quiet crying in the church, then in the end

Jamina and Albertina really started wailing loudly. Nyaga reckoned afterwards that that's how the Zulus cry when someone from the kraal dies.

It made me feel really lousy again, hearing all the bawling.

We were glad to get out of the echoing and into the hall, where we stuffed ourselves on tiny sausage rolls and everything else they'd been making when we were banned from the kitchen. While no one was watching, we stuck a few extra tarts and things into our pockets for later.

That afternoon I remember something had told me we wouldn't be staying at Oakdale much longer. We'd just broken up for Easter. And it was going to be our last holiday on the farm, I could just tell. It had hit me like someone casting lead into my guts, and I couldn't stop thinking about it. I had to do something. Get out or anything to stop myself from thinking about it.

"Phocho," I'd said, scanning the ridge, "let's go on a mission up Porcupine Hill and see if there are any new quills at the big hole." I didn't let on that I thought it might be our last chance of going up there, but I think he knew.

"Yah. And Lex? We take him too and see if he's lucky with the rabbits this time."

I'd had to laugh. He refused to believe that the wild rabbits could outrun an Alsatian.

We'd pulled our jeans and normal shirts on and took off, flicking through the seedy lucerne fields down towards the river. Lex went crashing through the rushes, vacuuming the ground with his nose as usual, following the mystery trails of duiker, dassies, rabbits, rats and maybe even porcupines, although they usually stuck to the forest higher up.

We were headed for the wattle plantation at the top of the hill where Lex had come a definite second against a porcupine once. He'd got quills in his face, front legs and chest, and was in a pretty bad way for a while. You'd think it would have taught him a lesson, but he still hunted them. Maybe he was out to get his own back.

"I'm glad we got away from all those tea-drinking dino-saurs," I said as we picked our way through the swampy mush.

"E-hey!" Phocho laughed.

Then suddenly he yelled out, balancing on one foot, flailing like a windmill. "I lost my shoe!"

It was my turn to chuckle as I slooshed through the farty mud to help him get it back.

"Look at you!" I hooted.

He tried to look at himself, nearly toppled over, then looked back at me plaintively, waving his flippers like mad. He was a crazy comic, old Phocho. You just had to laugh at him. He looked like a stork trying to imitate the leaning tower of Pisa, only he couldn't keep still. Then with a nervous cry he started to fall and had to put his foot down, plunging a clean sock into the stinky mud. That really got me going. I just went nuts, laughing, screeching at him, and waving my arms about while he looked back at me, more miserable than a kitten in a puddle.

Then I slipped. Onto my backside, with a horribly wet "flup!"

Phocho erupted. He shook and howled with laughter, in that real "serves you right" way, pointing one moment and clutching his stomach the next. We looked at each other for a moment, then burst out again till eventually there were tears, then we laughed at the tears, then at the foot covered in mud, the pants, the shoe buried in the mush, then at each other again till our stomachs screamed out, but the runaway train just wouldn't stop. And we didn't want it to, the laughing pain was too wonderful.

Lex just thought we were mad and carried on sniffing through the hairy grass on the other side.

Somehow we made it through the mush with battle-beaten shoes (and other bits) and started climbing the hill.

It was quite a mountain once you were on it. From a distance it looked okay, but that's just because your eyes don't have to do the climbing.

The mud soon came off our shoes as we puffed our way up the grassy slope, round the rocks that dotted the ground like Tim's big brother's pimples. Luckily the sky had clouded over and a cool breeze blew down into our faces, otherwise we would have been boiling and sweating from the effort. Some days it got so hot during the climb that we felt like giving up, but usually we'd gone too far to surrender before reaching the top.

Suddenly Lex dashed off to our left, whipping through the grass, his head down and ears back, dodging the boulders.

"He's seen something!" Phocho shouted. "There's it!"

A grey hare had darted out from behind a low rock. It leapt over a tuft and shot along the ground, swerving this way and that.

"Get him Lex! Get him boy!" Phocho cheered.

"They do that so that you can't hit them," I said.

"Eh?" Phocho looked puzzled.

"When you're hunting. They dodge like that so you can't shoot them."

"Ohhh."

The chase had disappeared round the slope, so we carried on climbing, looking with extra-keen eyes for more rabbits. It's mad how the search only starts properly once you've already seen one. It's like fishing. Sometimes down at the dam we'd get cheesed off because the bass just wouldn't be biting. We'd try spinners for a while and have no luck and get bored and start skimming stones or something. Or we'd have competitions to see who could hit a tree first, or even try throwing at white-eyes, but they were too fast for us. Then suddenly a fish would jump, and it'd be action stations, just about falling over each other trying to get to our rods for the first cast. We'd stop messing around and cast carefully into the good spots instead of aiming at floating twigs and things with our lures. And if nothing happened with spinners, we'd try other lures, like Lazy Ikes, or Rapalas, until we got something.

A short way on Lex came panting towards us, all bright

and bouncy, trying to pretend he'd caught it but didn't feel like showing us. His tongue lolled out almost to ground level as he puffy-hissed like a steam engine.

"You think he got it?" Phocho asked hopefully.

I snorted, and a dull ache reminded me of our laughing fit in the stream.

We walked on in silence, watching the sky ahead turning dark for the afternoon storm. The clouds moved in silently, packing shoulder to shoulder, whispering plans to catch the two idiots and the dog with everything they could muster. But we weren't scared of rain, we just kept on climbing.

By the time the slope started levelling out towards the top we were pretty sweaty, even though the sun had stopped trying. Phocho looked up at the sky, letting his mouth hang open like a fly-catcher.

"It's going to rain again," he observed, with the foresight of a true genius.

"Yeah."

"We stop for a rest?"

"We're nearly there," I said, "so let's stop right at the top."

But it was actually a lot further than we thought. That always happens. You think you've almost made it because you can't see much more ahead of you, but when you get to where you thought the top was, you realise there's still a hell of a lick to go.

Eventually we had to stop. We hadn't quite reached the highest point, but the plantation wasn't far off, so we flopped onto a flat rock, facing back down the slope. In silence we admired our handiwork. Or should I say footwork? Far below us the miniature red roof of our house nestled between the oaks, and beyond lay the pig sties.

"The second biggest pig farm in Natal," I said dramatically, as if I was in a trailer for a big movie.

Phocho studied the land spreading out below him, a frown of concentration on his face. And we didn't say another thing. My last words repeated in our heads over and over, getting more serious each time, then starting to sound silly until they finally lost their meaning altogether.

We stared at the dark landscape cowering beneath the heavy roof in the sky as the wind shepherded its swirling flocks.

I cleared my throat, but Phocho didn't move. We each knew the other was there, so there was no need to look. Or talk. Usually we had the same thoughts anyway. Often we'd start saying the same things at exactly the same time. It happened so much, we hardly got excited about it any more.

There was a soft crackle in the sky, like the storm person shifting his chair slightly before starting the show. The easy breeze had grown stronger, building all the time as the grass bent and rustled.

Lex sat next to me, also watching, his gentle panting drowned by the sound of the wind as it stirred the dark petticoats of the wattles, scaring the trees with its rising fury. Waving grass tickled at my ankles, then the darkness cracked loudly above. The horizon lit up in a nervous flicker, and a cold drop hit my elbow.

The first fat drops ticked onto our rock and the sky rumbled menacingly. Then a hissing sound crossed the grass behind us. It was the rain coming down with full force. In seconds it was upon us, the trigger we'd been waiting for.

"Let's get under the trees," I yelled.

Phocho was already on his feet, and we headed for the dark shelter beneath the wattles. Thunder cracked and boomed above, and lightning bleached the grass in front of us as we ran.

Lex reached the forest first. We climbed through the fence, hurried to the nearest tree and stood gasping for breath, hugging the gnarled trunk, listening to the heavy plopping around us as our bodies steamed the water from our clothes. The ground was dry beneath the tree, while outside the grassiness had faded behind a forest of water.

Minutes later the rain had slowed down to a lazy pace, so we took off deeper into the plantation towards the porcupine hole, looking for skulls and quills and things. Nothing lived in the hole any more, but neither of us had the guts to crawl down it. No bet could lure us down there.

We must have been about a minute away from the hole when I caught a movement from the corner of my eye. It was a big, silent shadow-dash from one tree to the next.

An ice-trigger chilled my spine.

I grabbed Phocho by the arm. Sensing my fear, he froze in mid-step. My flesh crawled slowly as I strained my eyes against the deep darkness of the forest. Something was there. Something big.

"What's it?" Phocho whispered.

"Sh!"

Drops landed nervously here and there, spoiling our chances of hearing anything. Then there was a movement again.

"There!" I hissed.

A shadow moved between two trees, then shifted out of sight, much deeper into the forest than before. It looked like a giant man, but it was hard to see in the darkness. My heart raced and witch's fingers tickled the back of my neck.

"*Ay!* Let's go," Phocho quavered.

"Quick!"

We turned in panic and sprinted the way we'd come, stealing urgent glances to see if it was after us. Twigs cracked underfoot, scaring us all the more, and leaves whipped our faces as we raced for the fence. My throat burnt, but there was no stopping. At last the twisted wire shone ahead in the light of the low sun. We burst through to the safety of the wet grass, our hearts desperately pounding to keep up.

We looked at each other wide-eyed for a while, catching our breaths. Then Lex emerged from the trees, keenly sniffing as if nothing had happened.

"And where were you just when we needed you?" I yelled.

He looked up with bright eyes and carried on panting. Sometimes I wish dogs could talk. I bet he'd seen the thing in the forest too.

"Did you see it?" I asked Phocho.

"I . . . I think so." His face was washed out. "It was horrible, *horrible!* Big *tokoloshe* thing down between the trees." His hand quivered as he fingered his necklace. He always fiddled with it when he got a fright.

"Yeah," I said, wondering if my eyes had deceived me. I didn't know what I'd seen. Phocho didn't know either. And suddenly I couldn't remember anything other than the running. Or whether I'd seen anything at all. In the sunlight it was hard to believe what had just happened. It was like waking from a nightmare, back to the normal world.

I don't believe in ghosts or anything, but that was the weirdest experience I ever had. It was only afterwards that I remembered Dad had died in the hills. Then I shivered at the thought. Maybe ghosts did exist. Maybe it was Dad trying to tell us something and we just ran away. But then again, I was probably just seeing things. At least that's what he used to say. He reckoned when people saw ghosts it was all in the mind. He called it auto-suggestion, whatever that means. So he could hardly have become a ghost if he didn't believe in them himself.

We didn't feel too comfortable going back down again, I can tell you. Every rustle made us jump, and we couldn't stop looking round to see if we were being followed.

"Lex!" I kept calling, "here boy!" I wanted him close, just in case.

Then we started to run again. As the slope got steeper, we went faster and faster. Lex thought it was great fun charging round boulders alongside us. He didn't seem to realise we were powered by the ghost of fear. Finally Phocho lost control and fell to the ground with a thump, just missing a rock and sliding through the grass. I managed to stop myself about a hundred steps later and turned to see him back on his feet again, racing down as if he'd just seen the devil.

"Wait for me!" he shouted, his eyes wild with fear.

"Hurry!" I urged, getting all jittery.

We didn't even stop for the stream at the bottom, tramping desperately through the mud, splatting all over the show, and sprinting on up to the house. We collapsed on the verandah, gasping with burny throats while our hearts bumped away like wild things.

Mom didn't need to hear about what we saw, so when we recovered we went down to the sties to talk about it.

We sat on the usual feed box in our favourite piglet refuge. Phocho picked his traditional 'discussion' straw from the thatch and chewed on it seriously as we chatted. After a while the piglets plucked up the courage to come through and chew at our shoes. We pinched absently at their noses as we talked.

"So you don't believe in ghosts, *Mafuqwane?*" He often called me by my Zulu nickname, which meant "he who walks fast". Should have meant "he who runs fast" after that little show, I reckon.

"I didn't used to," I said, "but I don't know what we saw in the forest if it wasn't one."

"Yah, same here." He chewed for a bit. "We should have stayed to have a better look, eh, what you say?"

It's funny how easy it is to be brave about something afterwards.

We almost decided to go back up for another look, but then we decided that we were tired and it was too late in the afternoon. Actually the truth of it was we were too chicken to go anywhere near there again.

"Eey, here's a blue-brown," Phocho observed, rubbing the forehead of a slightly runty piglet. Blue-browns were our favourites. They had one blue eye and one brown one. It was a sort of rule with us that we gave them special treatment because they were so rare.

After talking it over, we decided never to tell anyone about the thing on the hill, in case it decided to come and get us one day.

Chapter 3

Moving on

The farm had actually belonged to a firm in Greytown, which came as a horrible surprise to me. I'd always thought we owned the place. The pigs and things were ours, but the house and land were rented property, so we had to sell up the stock and move to wherever Mom could get a job.

Jenny had cried when she heard, of course, because she didn't want to leave all her connections. So to try cheering her up (and myself), I told her we'd just have to find a job for Mom in Greytown. It was easy to say at the time, but I knew there wasn't much work going in Greytown. It was a bit of a dump really. The thought of having to leave was pretty lousy, but Mom didn't need two howling brats to add to her problems, so I just kept quiet and hoped, while Jenny kicked up a noise and moped.

I found myself holding thumbs, even though I didn't believe in that sort of jaboosh, and whispering to myself, "Please let Mom find a job, please let us stay here." Pathetic, really, but the things you do when you get worried are a bit stupid. I didn't want to leave Phocho to look after Standard Five all on his own. He was the only real friend I had.

When we went to the trading store, I even had the cheek to ask Mr Barnes whether he needed Mom to help him out. That's how desperate I was. Of course he didn't need anyone, but he said he was looking out for something, just like all our other friends were. Then, after weeks of worry, Uncle Ray got the office job for Mom.

"Michael, Jenny, I've got some good news!" she'd reckoned after putting the phone down. I remembered noticing her eyes actually looking bright and hopeful again for the first time in ages. "Uncle Ray has found me a good secretarial job."

"Yeeeha!" I whooped, taking Jenny by the arms and swinging her around. "See Jenny, I told you not to worry!"

Then she'd continued: "There's only one snag, I'm afraid . . ."

"What's that?" I'd known what was coming before she said it.

". . . It's in Cape Town."

I just about dropped Jenny.

"But that's thousands of miles away!"

"Uncle Ray's found a nice house for us, something we can afford in the southern suburbs, and he says it's next to a very good school, so that's enough of your nonsense. You'll be able to meet plenty of new friends."

"But I don't want new friends," Jenny howled, "I want to stay with Carla and Melanie."

I'd felt slightly sick. It was the end of Greytown. We wouldn't be able to come visiting from so far away. No more riding. No more hunting and fishing. No more Phocho. And butterflies had panic-time inside me when I thought of the big city. I'd learnt about it in geography, but we'd never been anywhere near the place. I suppose in a way I was secretly excited, because it had a mountain and it was next to the sea, but at the same time I knew we'd never see home again.

I'd known Phocho all my life. I couldn't face making new friends, it sort of scared me. To tell the truth, I didn't really know how to do it. At the farm school you just knew everyone anyway.

Of course the news of our move had been big stuff at school the next day. Everyone reckoned they were jealous about us going to a city and all, which made me feel a bit better about the whole thing. Maybe it really would be fun. At least I'd be able to play soccer for a school that could make up a full team, and probably with real jerseys, socks and boots as well. I'd always fancied myself as a bit of a soccer player, but that was probably just because most of the other players at the farm school were pretty useless.

Even Jenny started to get quite keen on the whole idea. She started telling all the lighties about how she was going to suntan on the beaches and go board-sailing with a wet suit just like we'd seen them doing on TV.

I told Phocho we'd be able to go on huge missions up the mountain when he came down to visit us, and got all keen on the idea for a bit. Then he looked at the bad side, like he so often did, and said, "You'll have other friends over there. White friends to go on missions with. Nyaga hasn't money to send me so far away."

"Rubbish," I said, "we're best friends forever, remember? We're gonna start our own pig farm one day. That's still the plan, isn't it? It doesn't matter that we'll be so far away."

"Yah, *Mafuqwane*," he said, sort of dejectedly.

"Listen man, we're only going for a while until we can save up to come back. Then we can carry on where we left off. In the meantime we can write to each other. I'll send you photos of our new place and tell you all about it, and you can tell me all the news from home, so I'll feel just about the same as being here."

It's funny how easy it is to make plans like that, but usually they don't work out so smoothly. I knew deep down that we'd probably never come back, but I didn't believe it because it was too horrible to think about. So we made a sort of pact thing by putting our hands on top of each others' in a pile of four and saying with serious voices that we'd always be best friends, and that one day we'd get our pig farm together. Phocho also said that he'd work afternoons and weekends to get money for the train to Cape Town. And I reckoned I'd try and get a job to help out a bit as well.

We felt pretty good after that.

On the way home from school we'd made all sorts of plans about what we'd do in Cape Town in the holidays. Jenny kept throwing in her five cents worth about surfing and things, and we didn't even tell her to shut up. I suppose we were all trying to be as kind as possible to each other because we were leaving.

I kicked the dust on the path and looked very closely at the ground as we walked. It wasn't worth telling Phocho, but I was studying everything carefully as if it was the last time I'd ever see it.

I'd never realised how beautiful the gumtrees looked until that day. Towering up against the blue. I stared at the peeling bark, dark against the trunks which glowed in the blazing light. And suddenly the Christmas beetles were making beautiful music, their friendly rasping notes were like a never-ending orchestra. It was a sound you got so used to that you only noticed it when it stopped. Then it would be so quiet, your ears would carry on ringing from the silence.

We passed through the shadows of the gums and Phocho turned off towards the compound.

"See you tomorrow," he said heartlessly.

"Yeah, check you at the crack of dawn." I tried to be cheerful but it wasn't easy.

I walked on very slowly with Jenny holding onto my belt, not saying a word. There wasn't much fun in going home because we had to help with the packing as soon as we got there.

The hills of swaying plantations looked very special that day, and if I close my eyes I can still see them quite clearly in my mind.

Well, I must say the last few days before the weekend weren't too much fun. Phocho became more sulky each day at school until we even had a bit of a fight about it. It wasn't a bad rumble, and we soon made friends again, but it was pretty lousy for our last week together. Then every arvy we packed and tidied, and had to throw out all sorts of things that I'd collected. Mom reckoned we couldn't afford to take junk with us, so I argued that skulls and rare stones weren't junk, but it was like arguing with a brick wall. I found some really embarrassing old diaries I'd kept when I was ten, and took them to the kitchen stove and burnt them while no one was looking. Then straight afterwards I wished I hadn't done it because, even though I was such a wally in those days, there were some fantastic memories of all the things we used to get up to, and I'd just sent them all up in smoke.

Then on the Saturday morning, while it was still dark, the huge furniture lorry arrived. Phocho had slept over and we jumped out of bed to watch them loading up. It was amazing how quickly they got everything in. They used sacks to lift things with, and just zipped in and out like ants moving eggs out of a nest until the whole lot was done. Our beds went in complete with blankets still on. We had quite a laugh at that.

Phocho cheered up a lot in all the excitement and we had some good old-time laughs again. I said I was going on an extra long mission in a Lancaster and transferring to another air base. He said he'd keep the squadron under control at home, and we'd keep each other informed of our missions in regular briefings.

It might sound funny to you, but we spent just about the whole time pretending we were in the Second World War. It was from reading too many war comics, I suppose. At least that's what Dad used to say. He reckoned we were a blood-thirsty bunch. But we weren't really, we didn't believe in war and killing and stuff. It was just that it must have been quite scary and exciting if you always stood a chance of being shot down. Sometimes we pretended to get shot down, but we always managed to get home somehow. We were never taken prisoner or killed or anything. Everywhere we went was some bombing mission or other.

My rather fossilised grandpa was a Spitfire pilot in the Battle of Malta, and we always used to try and get him going with his war stories. He was actually shot down three times, and he's still got some cockpit glass in his hand from one of them. To tell the truth, I reckon he was pretty lucky to have got out of the war alive.

When the time came to say goodbye, we spoke in radio language complete with rogers and over-and-outs, which kept us from feeling too sad about the whole thing. Mom took off jerkily in the old farm bakkie and we bumped along Oakdale's driveway for the last time.

I looked out the back window and saw Phocho walking off with Lex, who was going to live with Nyaga at the compound. I wanted to cry, but Jenny would have thought I was a real naff, so I held it in. We thought it would be nicer for Lex to stay in the countryside he loved so much. It was hard leaving him behind, but we knew it wouldn't have been fair to take a big farm dog like him to the city. Phocho raised his arm and waved until we wound out of sight, swallowed by the trees that lined the stony track.

It took us two days to get to Cape Town, stopping in a pathetically ramshackle dump of a place somewhere in the Karoo for the first night. There was a biltongy old man in the dining room the next morning who had Jenny and me in stitches. Jenny called him a grasshopperman, and I must say he did look a bit like a locust, so we couldn't stop chortling the whole way through breakfast, until Mom got really cheesed off with us.

By the time we got to Uncle Ray's in Cape Town, we were sick to death of travelling, especially because we'd been squashed up three in the front of a bakkie all the way.

Playing games with car number plates soon wears off when you're only playing against your mom and lightie sister. I wanted to sit in the wind at the back, but Mom wouldn't let me, so I had to put up with Jenny whining all the way about how much further we had to go. So I pretended I was the navigator, working out how fast we were flying by checking the kilometre reading against my watch every five minutes. But I soon got sick of that too.

Then of course we got lost when we got to Cape Town and ended up having to phone for directions.

We spent the first night at Uncle Ray's, listening to him and Aunty Betty telling us all about their overseas trip, and showing us photographs of snow and boring old churches and things. Jenny ran off and played with my brat cousins while I looked at their tropical fish and read some of a crummy old Hardy book I'd already read long ago.

Next day Uncle Ray took us round to our new house.

It was really measly. No wonder Mom had thrown out all my valuables. There wasn't really room for much more than about three sardine-type people. We had a horrible time unpacking things and washing this, scrubbing that, helping Aunty Betty here, helping Mom and Uncle Ray there, fetching this, carrying that, it never seemed to end. It looked odd, all the things I knew so well suddenly in a different house. Everything in a sardine tin.

"That's enough now, Michael," Mom warned me, "this house is perfectly suitable for us, so stop your nonsense." I felt a bit guilty then, because I knew she was really tired and it was the best we could manage. "Why don't you take yourself and Jenny out from underfoot and go for a little walk while we have our tea?"

"Excellent!" I shouted. I was dying to have a look round, but we'd had to help first. "Come on, Jenny, you're an Albatross and I'm a Sunderland. Lets go on a reconnaissance flight!"

"I don't wanna be a Albatross," she whined.

"Okay, you're also a Sunderland, let's go!"

We took off, flying along at zero feet to avoid enemy radar, and headed up the road towards a park with soccer fields and real goal posts that I'd spotted on our way in. It wasn't all that long before we were leaning over the fence, just about drooling at a most beautiful sight.

There, before our simple farmer-type eyes, were three beautiful, bright green soccer fields with short grass, all neatly marked out with that proper white chalky stuff. It was

34

almost too good to be true. The only fields I'd ever played on had potholes and boulders, and grass that just about hid the ball from view. And suddenly there I was, casting my eyes over clean white goal posts with crossbars and proper supports.

A river lined with deep green trees wound its way along the far side of the fields, turning towards us and under the road alongside the third pitch. At the top end there was quite a larney clubhouse, and near the road at the bottom, almost swallowed by trees, a rusty corrugated iron shack with a small, dark window. Outside its hanging door, a can with a wire handle bubbled on an open fire.

At that stage I had a feeling I was going to enjoy living in the city, sardine tin or not.

"How's this, eh?" I said to Jenny as if she were Phocho, "flippin' excellent, eh?"

"I'll tell Mommy that you swore," Jenny sulked.

"Then I'll make you an Albatross again," I warned.

"You won't!" she shrieked. She didn't even know the difference between an Albatross and a Sunderland anyway.

"Okay, okay," I tried to stop her from exploding, "I won't, and I promise not to swear again if you don't tell Mom."

"I'm *not* a Albatross."

"Okay, okay, you're not an Albatross, you're a great big four-prop Sunderland."

She smiled her approval.

"Nice fields, eh?"

She didn't answer. I couldn't blame her really, she wasn't exactly all that interested in soccer, even though her brother was the Ace of Oakdale, ahem!

Somehow, Jenny wasn't exactly the ideal replacement for Phocho. I mean, what kind of a friend goes and tells on you just for a feeble swearword that isn't even good enough to be called a swearword anyway?

"Look at that old *khehla*," Jenny said, pointing back across the third field.

An old black man with the longest white beard I'd ever seen had emerged from the shack to inspect the fire. Even from that distance I could see how frayed his coat was, and his trouser legs hung down over his shoes just like a cart horse. He disappeared inside again with the steaming tin.

"What do you think he's doing?" asked Jenny.

"I don't know. S'pose he's having his supper. He's got a weird beard, eh?"

"What's weird?"

I looked at Jenny and sighed a real "oh kid sister" kind of sigh. "Strange, you know, sort of . . . odd."

"Oh."

She reached out and held onto my little finger. I smiled at her.

She was a real pain in the arse sometimes, but she was really not too bad when it came to little sisters.

Chapter 4

Pig

I did ask Francis about soccer first thing on the second day, but he said you couldn't join the team unless you'd been at the school for at least two years.

Suddenly I realised how much I really wanted to play in the team. Specially when I found out that they played on the fields at the soccer club. Once it was out of reach I really wanted it. But of course I pretended not to care.

"Well, I don't really like soccer all that much anyway," I lied, "an' I probably wouldn't have been good enough for the team."

"Goodenough! Ha ha ha," Francis roared, pointing at me.

Really clever stuff. Sometimes he was okay and then sometimes he changed into a member-of-the-gang type of bloke.

We were unpacking our things in the classroom before assembly when Hedley Bloumeyer turned up with his soccer ball. The moment he arrived, there was a big commotion as they started picking teams to play on the asphalt netball fields at break. So I hung around nearby, hoping someone would pick me. But they didn't even bother to look my way. They even picked some of the blokes who weren't there, saying "we book Richard," and "we've got Leon when he comes!"

I decided it was time to stop being a naff and speak up for myself. After all, if I couldn't be in the proper team, it would be my only chance of playing any soccer at all.

So I revved up some courage, took a deep breath and said, "Can I play?"

The buzzing voices suddenly stopped.

All heads aimed at me. I felt like melting away into the belting silence in my ears. I sat on one of the front desks as casually as possible, but everything I did felt forced and uncomfortable.

Nobody seemed to know what to say, and their eyes drilled into me until I thought I'd die, so I added rather weakly, "I play on the right wing . . ."

Trevor coughed.

"Well, you see," Mally mumbled vaguely, "we've . . . we've got even numbers." He'd hit on a good excuse and his eyes brightened up. "We've got seven a side, and it wouldn't be fair if one team had more players than the other."

I suppose he had a point, but we never bothered about odd teams at the farm school. Even the girls used to play with us.

Mrs Harvey's face appeared at the door, "Come on, Standard Fives, you don't need all day to unpack your things. Hurry up and get out."

There was an uncomfortable silence as we moved to the door. Somehow I'd destroyed the excitement by asking to play. But why should I have cared? They'd bloody-well destroyed mine, that's for sure.

Then, during the morning, I discovered I was in luck. We were already about halfway through maths when I noticed that Leon was absent. My heart quickened as I realised it meant they'd be a player short at break time. Then they'd have to give me a game. And I'd show them how well I could play down the wing. It would be difficult on the rather measly netball fields, but still I'd show them.

My mind started to go on tour again, the way it had in geography and had nearly got me taking the rap the day before. This time I could see myself racing down the touch line with the centre shouting for a cross. I kicked a well-judged, head-height pass to Trevor, who dived forwards and found the net, as they say in the soccer comics. The crowd erupted like chips in boiling oil. Then Trevor yelled, "Good one!" patting me on the back, "we've got to have you on the wing."

Mr Laing was looking in my direction, but I'd already learnt to keep an eye open for him. I pretended to have been puzzling over one of the volume problems he'd set us.

Francis looked over my shoulder to see how to do the third one. So I helped him, even though a part of me wanted to elbow him out of the way. He wasn't such a bad chap really, at least not when you compared him with the others. It was just a bit funny the way he'd be okay to me in the classroom, but didn't seem to even know me out at break.

"How many matches have you played this season?" I asked him quickly when Mr Laing's back was turned.

"Only three so far. The season's just started. We're playing Westridge this afternoon, away."

"How many've you won?"

"None so far."

"Eh?" I was surprised. Somehow I couldn't understand a team with such good fields being able to lose their games.

"What were the scores?"

"We lost the first one five-nil, then we nearly won the second game one-nil, but the stinking crook of a ref didn't blow the final whistle until his team had scored twice, so we lost that match two-one . . ."

"Who scored?"

"Trevor."

I shouldn't have asked. He seemed to do everything in that place.

"That ref was a bloody crook . . ."

"What position does he play?"

"Eh?"

"Where does Trevor play?"

"Oh, centre forward.

So my little daydream had been pretty accurate in one way. Now all I had to do was to put in an amazing cross at break and it would be perfect.

"And the last game?" I whispered.

"Five-two."

"Who scored? Trevor again?"

"He got one, from a penalty, and Richard got the other one. Richard's pretty good. He plays in the midfield, but mostly he ends up helping the backs."

"Why's that?"

Francis sighed and looked at me as if I was really thick or something. "Because the other teams are just about professionals compared to us."

"Why's that?"

"Because they've got so many players to choose from, and they've got proper coaches an' everything. We've just got old Drac, who doesn't know a bloody thing about soccer: 'Run round the field; do push-ups; stop bunching,' that's all he can say. I reckon the old coon could give us better training."

"Coon?"

"Some old Af who hangs around the fields and cleans up sometimes."

Mr Laing towered over us. "Any problems?"

Francis looked at him through the top of his head. "No sir."

"Well, let's have more work and less chit-chat, shall we?"

"Yes sir."

The break bell drilled away in the quad and we dived for the door. Everyone was in such a hurry to hit the netball fields, I didn't know who to ask, so I just shouted, "I'll take Leon's place!"

Nobody seemed to hear.

"I'll play in place of . . . oh, what the hell . . ."

I gave up because no one was listening, and chased them down to the field, my heart pounding all the way.

"Can I play for Leon?" I panted once on the netball field.

Mally swivelled round, his eyes wide with "What are we gonna say to him now?" written in them.

Then Trevor reckoned, "Only soccer people can play."

"Yeah, only soccer people can play," the others echoed.

I tried to protest. "But the teams won't be even."

"Terry's gonna play."

"But he's a Standard Four," Alexander objected.

"Shut up!"

"He's played for the team before."

"Yeah, he's been picked for the team before," they chorused.

"But he's useless," the same voice chirped.

"Shut up."

It was unbelievable. I turned away in disgust as they called Terry over and Andy started the game by making a childish whistle noise with his voice.

They were even prepared to take on a Standard Four to keep me out of the game. I felt sick. At first I sat down to watch, but then I decided not to pay them that compliment, and got up to leave.

I walked around the prefabs and through the quad where I saw Jenny skipping with some other girls, so I quickly changed course before she noticed that I was on my own. I hung around the cricket nets for a while, sitting on a rotting old log that they obviously used as wickets, until too many lighties started staring at me, so I got up and moved on.

At the bottom end of the hall there was a narrow alleyway where they put all the rubbish bins out. There was no one around, so I sat down for a bit and wondered what Phocho was doing at that exact moment. He probably thought I was playing a steaming game of soccer and making piles of friends and things.

Huh.

From where I sat, I could hear the shouts from the netball field as they called for the ball or cheered for goals and argued whether the shot was too high or not. They were just out of sight round the side of the hall. Each shout made me sicker and sadder.

They were the biggest bunch of wallys I'd ever met.

My mind started toying with various tortures and things that I'd dish out to them if I had my own way, until I started to feel a bit guilty about it. If they ever wanted to do anything with Phocho and me, we'd just laugh in their faces, that was a definite thing. I wouldn't take any of those stinking rats on holiday to Greytown with me, that's for sure.

There was a thud on the wall nearby, then the ball rolled and bounced into my alleyway, followed by the sound of running feet. I jumped up, scrambled behind the bins and hit cover just in time to avoid being seen.

The mystery ball-fetcher came gasping down the gutter and I froze myself into a bundle, not daring to breathe. I listened tensely as he picked the ball up, tried to kick it out (but it hit the eaves and bounced back), kicked again, then disappeared. I stayed squashed up for a while, then relaxed and realised how much I was shaking.

It was terrible hearing the game without seeing what went on, so I sneaked to the corner and watched through a bush, from behind some flaky sort of pinetree where I could see about half of the field. I was just in time to see Mally miss-kick a spinning ball. He meant it to go forwards, but it glanced off his foot and skidded sideways along the hard surface, falling at Richard's feet. Richard looked quite good, the bit of him that I saw before he dribbled it out of sight. Trevor was playing into the goal at my end, with Mally on the right wing where I'd imagined myself playing. I rubbed my hands together, thinking about how Mally had duffed that shot. The ball bounced into view again from a goalie's kick, and Benjy chested it awkwardly to the ground just in time for Trevor to steam through and confiscate it. He dodged a defender and sent a blistering shot just wide of the jersey to doof loudly against the wall.

"Miss!"

Maurice placed the ball and took a goal-kick.

I didn't really want to torture anyone. I just wanted to play soccer too.

When Leon came back the next day, I knew there was definitely no chance of me getting a game with them.

Sometimes I'd watch them play from the three steps where

spectators are supposed to sit, but mostly I'd hide behind the tree and check out who could play and who was useless.

Some of them were quite good, mainly Richard and Trevor, but the others weren't much to rave about. I reckoned I'd have been able to get into the school team all right if only I was allowed to play.

On the schoolwork front, things weren't going too badly I suppose, seeing that I had a whole stack of stuff to catch up.

Or at least, that was until we had to hand our projects in.

On my second day Mr Laing had given us a week to do a sort of mini-project thing about Insects and Arachnida, which is spiders and things. We had to write about the differences between the groups, illustrating them with diagrams of an insect and an arachnid. It counted for year marks, so he reckoned we had to do it properly or we'd be shot at dawn, hung, drawn and quartered.

We had until Tuesday to do it or die, and I'd spent the entire weekend catching up notes and things, so of course Mom nearly had a fit when she caught me attempting to knock off a whole project on the Monday night. But I finished it okay. Eventually. It was well after midnight when I collapsed into bed, but I must say it didn't look too bad the next morning. Or at least, it didn't look as if I'd churned it out in one go, and Mr Laing would never be able to tell.

But when I got to school and saw Amanda Pierce and Cheryl Moore comparing projects, I suddenly realised that they were in a totally different league from me. Their writing was painfully neat, and their pencil diagrams looked like big works of art, carefully coloured in with pinks and mauves and stuff. My writing was all scratchy and crooked, and I'd gone and done my crabby drawings in pen.

I sat through the morning lessons, worrying about year marks and things, and hoping that Mr Laing wouldn't call for the projects before break, so that I could fix mine up a bit then. I was in luck. The bell went and he hadn't called for them, so I asked Francis if I could borrow his pencil crayons. He looked slightly disgusted and reckoned I'd do better by asking one of the girls if I really needed some. The classroom emptied, leaving only Stella and Carol, who hung back to whisper about someone, as usual. That was about the worst choice I could have wished for. I suppose you could say they scared me, in a stupid way. And they were big mates with Trevor and the gang, so I decided to go and spy on the soccer instead.

By lunch-time I'd given up the idea of asking for pencil crayons. I don't know why, but I didn't want any of the girls to think I couldn't afford my own. Funny, that. Me not minding if Francis knew, but being so worried about the girls, even though I never spoke to them. So I decided I was just going to have to get a lousy year mark instead.

Towards the end of the day, all the soccer hackers were getting really wound up about their home game, because Tuesday was match day. They reckoned they were going to give this lot a hiding for a change, because they were supposed to have the worst A team in the league.

I was more worried about what Mr Laing would do to me for not colouring in my diagrams. So eventually I asked Francis about it.

"Naa, you don't have to colour them in," he reckoned. "The girls just do that because they're a bunch of suctions. We don't bother. Anyway, it's double geography till home time, an' Drac's such a doze-ball he's not gonna remember to ask for them now."

He said if I showed him mine, he'd tell me if it was okay. So I waited for Mr Laing to turn to the board and scribble something on his blob that was supposed to be Europe, then slid it out of my desk. I was just sneaking it open on my lap when . . .

"*Goodenough!*"

My hands crumpled with fright.

"What have you got there?"

All heads aimed at me in a deathly hush. I looked down at my mangled project, then slowly up at Mr Laing.

"Um . . ." What could I say? "My project, sir."

His face lit up. "Aaah! I nearly forgot! Thanks for reminding me, Goodenough. Right! All biology assignments out on your desks now, and hurry up, we're running out of time."

There were groans and muffled curses as people dug into cases and desks. All except Trevor. He just sat, checking me out with murder in his eyes.

Mr Laing breezed round the room, snatching up the projects, making sarcastic comments — like asking Celia Walker if her dog had helped her to write hers — and the same for Benjy, and congratulating George Fergadiotis and some of the girls. Then he got to Trevor.

"And where's yours?" Mr Laing asked very softly.

Trevor sat with his arms folded on the empty desk, stubbornly refusing to look up. "Forgot," he mumbled.

"*What*!"

"Forgot."

"Right, Surridge, this has gone far enough! You're staying here this afternoon, match or no match, and you're not leaving this desk until you've finished that project! You hear me?"

That made Trevor look up.

"But sir-"

"No buts! I'm sick and tired of your nonsense. If you'd wanted to play that badly, you'd have got your work done on time."

"But sir, I left it at home," Trevor protested.

You could tell he was making it up, and so could Mr Laing.

"Well that's just tough. You can start another one this afternoon."

Trevor checked me out. In fact, just about all the soccer blokes were checking me out. I looked down and pretended not to notice, and so did Francis.

I'd really blown it. I reckon they would have got me good and proper that afternoon if the whole team hadn't had to change straight after the bell. Apart from Trevor who had to stay in, that is. Everyone sort of bumped at me on their way out and reckoned under their breaths how lucky I was that Trevor couldn't get hold of me then.

And to make things worse, our team got beaten three-nil by the "useless bunch". In class the next day Francis told me they all reckoned it was my fault they lost, because Trevor wasn't there. And when the team had got back to change, Trevor's project was such a mess, he was told to do it again unless he wanted to get five per cent for his end-of-year mark.

I'd decided to keep well out of Trevor's way that morning, but to make sure it didn't look as if it was on purpose. At home, I kept Jenny waiting for as long as possible before we left for school. Then on the way I kept hanging back and wasting time till she got totally cheesed off with me. I stopped and pretended to be really interested in the flowers and things, telling her all about them and pretending to be amazed at how their colours had changed since the day before.

"But Jenny, can't you see how different the colour of these Wobulators has gone?" I was inventing the flower names and all, because Jenny didn't know any better.

"No."

"But you must be able to: they've gone so *blue*! I'm sure they must be being attacked by Arachnida."

"What?" Jenny got interested for a moment, but then she stamped, "Come *on*, we're going to be late!"

"Wait! Come back and look here, we might find some Arachnida . . ."

We got through the gates just as the bell went. Saved by the bell again.

Then, when little break began at the end of English, I took my life into my hands and asked Mr Stirling some stupid questions, about essays and whether it was a good idea to try using big words even if you weren't sure what they meant. I pretended not to notice Trevor and a few others waiting for me like vultures just outside the doorway, but Mr Stirling did.

"What are you boys doing here? Go on, be off with you!" Then he turned to me, not realising that he'd just saved my life. "Now, as I was saying, in some cases it depends how unsure you are of the word, for example . . ."

By the time he'd finished rambling on about big words, the others were sick of waiting, and well into their soccer match. At big break I did the same thing with Mr Laing, saying I wanted to check if my science notes were properly up to date, and then arranging to see him straight after school so that he could explain what the first term experiments had been about.

By Thursday I'd run out of excuses to slow Jenny down, but still managed to arrive about two minutes before the bell. Things seemed to have calmed down a bit. Or at least they had given up waiting outside doorways for me. But I still took my time getting out of the classroom each break, just to make sure that they'd kicked off before I got out.

Then on Friday, before school, quite an interesting thing happened. Mr Laing stopped me in the corridor and asked what sport I played.

I said "None." Then "sir," quickly, before he could bite my head off.

So he reckoned, "Why not?"

"Sir, because I've never played tennis," (I think it's a real naff's game, but I didn't say so) "and I'm not allowed to play soccer."

Those were the only sports I had to choose from, really, apart from judo, which was mainly for the lighties.

"Why, do you have an injury?"

"What . . . I mean, I beg your pardon, sir?"

"Why aren't you allowed to play soccer?"

"Because I haven't been here for two years. Sir."

"Where do you get that nonsense from?"

"I . . ."

"Can you play soccer?"

"Yes sir."

"Well, see to it that you turn up for Monday's practice down at the club fields. We need as many players as we can get. Haven't been here for two years, I ask you!" he snorted in disbelief. "Do you know where to go?"

"Yessir!"

My head fizzed like lemonade, I was so chuffed. Soccer practice! That was ace news.

So Francis had been spinning me a sprout-story all along. I couldn't wait to tell him I'd joined soccer, and to see his face as he realised he'd been found out.

I skipped off along the corridor and into the drizzle in the quad as if it was a gloriously sunny day, humming the chorus of a stupid song that always popped up when I was happy. I suppose that's why it's called pop music.

I told Francis that I knew he'd been sprouting, and he acted all innocent, as if it hadn't been a dirty trick to keep me out of the team. "Well that was the way it *used* to work," he said transparently. "Eh, Mally?"

"What?"

"There *used* to be a rule that you couldn't play for the team unless you'd been at the school for two years?"

"Oh," Mally sounded a bit lost, "yeah, I suppose so. I think it was, yeah."

That break I marched down to the netball field to join the regular match, without saying anything to anyone. As they sorted their teams out, I stood right in amongst them.

"What are you doing here? You aren't a soccer player," Andy reckoned, all challenging-like.

"I am now," I retorted like a real main ou.

"Since when?"

"This morning," Francis cut in. "Sir's told him to come to practice."

"Well I'm not having any pigs in my team."

"Yeah, and no pigs in our team either," Mally piped up.

"What?" I stammered in disbelief.

"You'll be telling tales to the ref next thing."

"Go'n play for some kaffir team," said Trevor. "Go'n get that piccanin friend of yours . . . and join Kaizer Chiefs!"

Everyone roared.

"We'd rather pick a girl than have a traitor like you playing for us," Leon chirped.

"Yeah!"

"Go'n feed your pigs," Andy added. "We don't need any farmers in our team."

"I'm not a farmer, I live here."

"You're still a pig, no matter where you live."

Everyone laughed and people started catching on to the pig idea.

"Yeah, Pig!" and "Go back to your pen!"

Then Trevor said, "Grunt off!"

There were gusts of vicious laughter. And the horrible thing was that I noticed even Francis was laughing with them.

I felt totally shot down in flames and hated myself for it. I'd flown straight over enemy guns and was stupid enough to think they wouldn't open fire.

I walked away with fists so tightly clenched, my fingernails cut into my palms. And the more laughing I heard, the more my nails cut, until the voices disappeared behind me.

I shook like an old fossil from being so cross and frustrated and miserable all at once. I felt so sorry for myself that I thought I'd howl any minute, right in front of all the lighties. I had to swallow hard and tried to think about deserts and things, but it was no good. I wanted to get out there and strangle them. I wanted to beat them at soccer, one against the rest. I know it sounds really pathetic now, but that's how stupid I get when I'm fuming mad like that.

To tell the truth, when I thought about them calling me Pig and telling me to join Kaizer Chiefs, I think I did kind of almost cry, but no one really noticed, so it didn't matter. It wasn't the first time they'd called me Pig. It had been sort of catching on ever since I mentioned the farm on my first day, but it hadn't really come out into the open as my official nickname before. But it was the first time they said anything about Phocho to me. Just because he was a Zulu. It reminded me of the Oliviers who took their stinking brats out of the school because of him. As if he was poison or something.

He was a bloody sight more decent than any of them, that's all I can say. In Greytown no one ever said "kaffir". It was like the worst swearword you could think of, but down here all the blokes couldn't care less. It means unbeliever, anyway, I looked it up in a dictionary once, so I don't know why they used it.

I parked off and moped about things on my own for a while, and I must say, apart from horrible things, the world seemed pretty much empty to me. There wasn't really anything in the world worth living for, when I got to thinking about it. So I thought about hanging myself and stuff. Maybe from one of the trees at the soccer club. Then when they came down for a practice, they'd see what they'd done to me.

They wouldn't ever be able to forgive themselves for driving me to suicide. Maybe they'd never say "kaffir" again. But it didn't take me long to decide against that one. I mean, why should I worry about a bunch of consolation prizes like them?

At big break they played stingers and, surprise, surprise, Andy actually asked me if I wanted to play!

I couldn't believe it. He was probably feeling a bit guilty about the soccer episode, because he'd started it really. I was so surprised by the sudden change of fortune that I said "Yes" before I even knew it.

I ran down to the tennis court with them, feeling like a champion and forgetting all the bad stuff, but also sort of embarrassed, as if everyone must have been noticing me because I didn't normally play.

We got into a circle and my feet tingled with the thought that in a matter of seconds I'd have to be running for my life, in a way. It was my first chance to show them that I was quite hot at stingers myself. I had to put on a good show.

We made a ring and started to fist the ball about to see who would be *on*. The first shot came straight for me, but I kept it safely away from my legs, punching it hard and straight towards Maurice, who blocked it just in time.

Quite a few shots came at me, and gradually I realised that just about everyone on the opposite side of the circle were trying to get me *on*. I didn't mind though, because they were giving me a bit of practice so that I could really get my eye in. Leon kept fisting straight at me, even though he wasn't actually opposite me, and that turned out to be his downfall, much to my amusement. Hedley shot the ball at him and he tried to knock it at an angle towards me, but mis-timed his swing, letting the ball shave his fist and ricochet between his legs. Everyone whooped and scattered as Leon picked up the ball and looked around like a tyrannosaurus.

I sensed he was looking for me and ducked behind George to avoid being noticed. Trevor ran towards Leon to tempt him into taking a shot, so he flicked a quick underhand throw that took Trevor by surprise, catching him under the chin.

"Aw," he groaned, and the rest of us cheered.

He noticed me cheering, and immediately I knew it had been a fatal mistake. His eyes lit up.

"Where's Pig?" he shouted, even though he knew perfectly well where I was.

"Get Pig!" Leon whooped, and suddenly I was the only target.

They passed and ran, getting closer to me to take a shot. My heart raced and my eyes were wide as I watched for the openings and took them. Trevor collected a pass right next to me, and as I ran to escape being branded, Mally bumped into me, knocking me to the ground.

"Oops!" he said as I grazed my knee on the tarmac, but I knew he'd done it on purpose. It wasn't half obvious. The ball flew past my ear at a steaming pace, so close that I felt the wind from it.

So their cheating didn't work.

Trevor ran after the ball as I picked myself up slowly. I'd

51

sort of lost the will to play because my grazed knee boiled and burnt with rawness, but they were still after me, so I had to run.

While I was watching Trevor with the ball, I ran straight into Leon, who clamped his arms round me and shouted, "Come and get him!"

"Hey," I protested, "that's not fair!" and I struggled to get loose.

He laughed, but it suddenly came to a choked full stop as my elbow jabbed into his stomach in my bid to escape. His grip on me tightened and I could sense that he'd lost his rag. He'd got all serious and was wanting to try and rumble with me, but he was a bit of a weed, so I could have handled it.

By that time Trevor had run all the way up to me (which is also crooking) and branded me a really hard shot that left a mark on my thigh. There were cheers and shouts, and Leon had to let me go because now I was also *on*.

Even though I wasn't in the mood for playing any more, I chased and cornered people, then shouted for the ball. But of course they didn't pass to me. They tried pathetic, long-range shots and anything they could, just as long as it meant not having to pass to me.

I didn't get a chance to take a single shot.

Once I collected the ball on the loose, but I was stupid enough to pass it instead of taking a shot, thinking it would teach them to pass to me. How thick to have thought it would have made any difference!

By the end of the game it was quite obvious that they'd only asked me to play so they could get a chance to brand me.

So that was my first and only game of stingers with them the whole term.

Chapter 5

Johannes

Getting Trevor into trouble was the worst thing I could have done, that had become pretty clear to me. And giving Leon the elbow during stingers didn't help things either. But there was another mistake that day that really put the cream on top.

The difference was, though, that this one was beyond my control. If I could have done anything about it, it would never have happened. I'd learnt better by then, but obviously Mom and Jenny hadn't.

Even though they pulled a sly one on me in that stingers game, I saw it as a decent step in the right direction with the blokes. Well at least it was, until Benjy's little sister in Jenny's class went and asked her why they call me Pig.

That was the end.

Of course I hadn't told anyone about my new, intelligent-animal-type of name. They would have taken it all the wrong way and wondered what was wrong with me if people thought I was a pig. Especially moms and aunts and things. They always worry about that sort of stuff so much, as if a stupid, childish nickname is going to worry you. I'd known that if Jenny heard it, she would run straight off to the management and split on me. And that's just what she did.

Mom had a half-day and fetched Jenny from school because the young lighties get out earlier than us, and I reckon the story was out before she even got in the bakkie.

I didn't know what was up at first, but I knew something was wrong because during supper Mom kept looking at me with this silly worried expression, as if I was sick or something. She'd been doing it a bit ever since she asked me about new friends and I'd told her that they were all bogeyheads. But on that Friday, Mom was really laying the worried-mother thing on a bit thick.

After a while I couldn't stand being stared at any more, so I said, "What?"

"How was school today?" she asked.

It was one of her usual interrogations, so I gave her the usual answer. "Fine."

"No problems with anybody?" She really looked worried.

"No. Why?"

"Jenny tells me that they're calling you Pig."

I turned on Jenny viciously. "Where did you hear that?"

"Angie Vermaak told me," she said, all conceited and proud of herself.

"Is it true?" Mom probed, obviously worried about the whole thing.

"Yeah, sort of I suppose."

"Why's that? Are they fighting with you?"

"No, it's just a feeble name, just because of the farm, I guess."

"So you aren't having any trouble then? What about that boy you were telling us about — Trevor — he's not causing problems for you?"

"No. Everything's fine," I said, a bit impatiently so that she'd stop asking all those stupid questions.

I could tell that she was still worried about it, but I pretended not to notice, and changed the subject. "Mr Laing said I can join soccer."

"Oh good!" Mom said, hanging onto anything slightly positive-sounding, and smiling for the first time since we'd started supper.

That should keep her quiet, I thought.

"Will you be needing boots?"

"No, the old ones still fit fine."

I wouldn't have minded new boots, but that would have

had her worrying about money as well as me, so I shut up about them.

On Monday, thinking back about the Pig story, I reckoned Mom had taken it quite well. Or at least I must have done a good job of convincing her there was nothing to worry about, because she didn't say another word on the subject the whole weekend.

As it turned out, I couldn't have been more mistaken.

That afternoon, all prepared for my first soccer practice and walking to the fields with the others, I saw Mom heading towards the school in the old rattletrap bakkie. As she passed us, she hooted and waved at me. I could have shrunken away, I felt such a wally. She was supposed to be at work, not driving around and embarrassing me.

"Is that your mom?" Trevor asked me.

"Yeah," I said, feeling a total chop.

"Larney car," someone commented, "kaffirmobile!" and everyone laughed.

I pretended not to hear, which was pretty feeble, seeing that everyone else obviously had. My face went red again, so I looked over the edge of the bridge down the railway line until I could feel it cooling down a bit.

At the field we kicked three balls around while we waited for Mr Laing to pitch up. I tackled and passed a bit to get used to the feel of the ball again, and even got passed to once or twice, which made me think maybe the blokes were going to get on with me at last, since I was also a soccer player. Come to think of it, it was mainly the Standard Fours who passed to me, but the others were okay too.

I might have been right, I don't know, but it made no difference, because at that very moment Mom and Mr Laing were busy changing all that anyway.

"He must be having his usual gallon of tea," Francis commented, as it got later and later.

Finally his grey mini arrived and we all cheered sarcastically. He whistled us over and picked Richard and Trevor out as captains to choose teams. I felt a nervous excitement brewing in my guts. At last they would have to pick me.

The words "at last" turned out to be truer than I expected. I was the last player to be picked, and it was Trevor who had to have me. That didn't worry me too much, though, because I knew I'd be able to prove my worth soon enough. That much I could tell from having watched the others on the netball field for so long.

Trevor was busy allocating positions to his team, so I reminded him I played on the right wing, in case he'd forgotten, but he said Mally always played there, and made me a defender. That was the kind of stinking treatment I'd expected anyway, so I didn't let it bug me. I'd soon show them, one way or another.

Mr Laing blew the whistle and my career of soccer on a real field began.

Mally and Trevor took the ball upfield and managed to force a corner, so our whole team crammed up into their box in the hope of scoring, leaving a dangerously open field for them to break away in, so I hung back near the halfway line just in case that happened. Richard's whole team was in the box to defend, so I was pretty much on my own in the middle of the field. No wonder Mr Laing always told them to stop bunching.

Zak took a wild boot at the ball to clear it downfield, but there was no one to chase it, so I ran up and intercepted it to bring it back into the attack. Benjy called for it on the left wing, and I sent a long, lofted pass to him just as two Standard Four lighties came to tackle me. It was a good pass, but Benjy lost the ball, so Mally shouted at me for not passing to him as we ran back in defence.

"Right," I thought, "next chance I get, I'll pass to you and let's see if you can do any better!"

We had a bit of a goalmouth scramble a few minutes later, and I managed to get the ball off Richard (which didn't go unnoticed by Mr Laing) and broke away on the right. Mally was up ahead, almost offside, screaming frantically for the pass.

"Right, here you are," I thought, "and I hope you lose it."

I sent the ball up ahead of him so that he didn't have to slow down, and Trevor raced down the centre with him. Mally dribbled a lightie defender, but then he lost control of the ball and it went out of play.

"Sorry," he said to Trevor who stood, frustrated, with hands on hips.

"Typical!" I thought, but secretly I felt really pleased with myself.

Mr Laing blew to stop the game for a moment.

"Goodenough, where do you normally play?"

"Me sir?" I was taken aback by the sudden attention to me.

"Yes, who else? You're the only Goodenough on the field, aren't you?"

"Yes sir. Um." (This was a bit dangerous, because Mally wouldn't be too pleased if he put me on the right wing. But then again, I reckoned, what did I owe to him?) "I normally play on the right wing, sir."

"All right. Mally and Michael, swop places."

"But sir . . ." Mally protested.

"You heard me!"

"Sir."

We trotted past each other, and Mally gave me an I'll-kill-you-for-this type of look.

The game restarted and for a while I had nothing to do. Mally made sure that none of his passes came my way, so everything happened down the left wing with Benjy.

The Standard Four lighties had nothing against me, but they hardly ever got the ball, so I had to rely on Francis for passes, because he was about the closest thing to a human being out of that whole gang of lenses. I collected a pass from him, but didn't control it properly, letting it run out of play, and I cursed myself viciously for being so stupid, for blowing one of my few chances. Of course Mally had a lot to say about how useless I was, as if he was the ace player himself or something. He just about blamed me for the fact that we were a goal down. I felt like reminding him it was only a practice, but thought better of it.

A bit later I got a pass from a lightie just inside our half and took it down the wing past two defenders. My heart beat up a commotion as I ran. I could see Trevor from the corner of my eye, and in a flash it dawned on me that my classroom daydream was coming true. As long as I didn't mess up the cross.

Trevor called for the ball at the top of his voice: "Pig! Here Pig!" he yelled.

As we reached the big box, I sent a beauty of a cross just beyond the last defender. It was all happening!

Then Mr Laing blew the whistle.

I couldn't believe it. Trevor wasn't offside. He was in a perfect position to score, and with only the weedy Maurice to beat.

"That's not offside sir," Trevor objected.

"That's not what I blew for," said Mr Laing, striding rather menacingly towards him. "If you call Michael Good-enough 'Pig' again, I'll personally wring your neck for you. Do you hear me?"

"Eh?" Trevor was just as surprised as I was.

"You heard me!" he bellowed.

"Sir." He looked at the ground sheepishly.

I didn't know what to do with myself. Everyone was staring at me in stunned silence. They probably thought I'd complained or something, because he didn't normally seem to worry about nicknames. He didn't stop them from calling Andy "Snolly". In fact, sometimes *he* even called him that.

Mr Laing bounced the ball to restart, but we'd lost the advantage by then, and they got a goal kick.

It was as we waited for Maurice to kick the ball back into play that I noticed the strange, wizard-like man with the long white beard whom I'd seen on the first day, watching us from the far side of the field.

"That's the coon boy," Francis said, startling me. He'd been standing right behind me and noticed me looking.

"Eh?"

"The old coon with the beard. He often watches us."

Maurice kicked a real duffer of a shot that rolled along the ground. I lunged forward, collected it and took a steaming kick at goal before he could get back into position. In my hurry I miscued the shot and hit the near post, but it landed perfectly for Trevor, who scored easily.

"Yay!" we all cheered.

Well, all but one of us. Mally looked on with poisonous eyes.

It was a good practice. Mr Laing told me to bring my boots to school for the match the next day. I'd either go on as a reserve or have a whole game against Boughton.

I must say that made me feel pretty full of zizz as I walked home. Even though I could sense that Mally had it in for me, and that maybe Trevor thought I'd run to Mr Laing about the Pig story, being in the team seemed to rule all that out.

On my way past the stream at the bottom of the grounds I thought I heard a hissing noise.

"Fsst!"

I stopped. It came from the bushes beside the stream. I looked carefully, then with a sudden shock noticed two strong brown eyes smiling at me. They were surrounded by a dark, weather-worn face. It was the wizard!

"*Molo mnumzana*," he said with a nod.

"*Sawubona baba*." I didn't know any Xhosa, so I spoke Zulu.

"*Hawu*! You speak Zulu!" He bounced with delight, pretty agile for someone his age. "You play good soccer and you speak Zulu! What's your name, *mnumzana*?" His clothes were pretty shoddy, but his face was really kind, and his beard made him look sort of wise and gentle.

"Mike."

"Miyke," he said thoughtfully. "I'm Johannes, very pleased to meet you, *mnumzana*."

He held out a rugged hand without moving from the bushes, so I had to duck under them and go to him to shake it. We did the triple handshake. He knew I'd know it.

"You new boy here?"

"Yeah, we came from Greytown."

"Greytown, ohhh . . . that's a *very* long way," he said, as if he'd been there himself.

"And you?"

"Me? Ohhh," he scratched at his chin, and the coarse beard hairs crackled under his nails, "I come from the Transkei. Once my boss took me to *Thekweni*, you know, Durban? And there I learn Zulu . . . but I was sad there, *very sed*! So I come back to Cape Town, and now I work here most of my life. Long time now, too long to remember!" He chuckled, and a wet weasel whistled in his lungs as he did so.

It was a sound similar to Nyaga's cough, which he reckoned came from smoking too much. He used to say that to put me off smoking, but it backfired because I liked the sound, which was quite funny. I didn't smoke anyway. Phocho and I tried once or twice smoking khaki weed, but it was even worse than Sipho's pipe tobacco rolled in newspaper which he always used to offer us.

"And the Transkei? Do you ever go back?"

"Ohh yah, when I get holidays, I go home to my wife and my family . . . July, you know, and Christmas."

He came out from under the bushes, where he'd been breaking up sticks for his fire. We walked towards his shack in silence. He threw some of the sticks into the flames, then sat on a well-worn, rounded rock, absorbing the warmth with opened hands.

I tried to imagine only seeing Mom and Jenny twice a year, but I couldn't. It was too lousy to think about.

"Hey? You only see them twice a year?"

"Yah. I must work down here in Cape Town. There's no work in the Transkei, no money." His eyes were distant for a second, then he turned back to me. "You sit for a time?" He indicated the rock next to his.

"Thanks."

Once I'd sat down by the fire, he rubbed his hands in satisfaction, breathing out loudly with a gaping mouth.

"You play good soccer, *mnumzana*. They need you. They need you to be the wing, they play bad games this year."

He made me feel quite important.

"Last year they had a good team . . . yah . . . good man playing centre," he clapped with delight, "you have to put him in a cage to stop him scoring goals." He laughed again, a huge mouth of teeth. "But this new one in the centre, what's he called?"

"Trevor."

"Yah, Trevor. He's not bad. Give him a chance and he's good. So far he's unlucky. Not enough passing from the other men . . . Now, there *you* can help."

"You think so?" I really felt flattered.

"Yah. You listen what I say, don't pass to those other *skelems* . . . pass to Trevor in the middle, and pass also to the firehead."

"Richard?"

"That good one, got red hair, you know which one?"

"Ah yeah, Richard. He's good."

"Yah. He's got good feet, the firehead *mnumzana*. Now you remember what I say. Pass to Richard, Richard and Trevor, and the team will be *good*!"

"I'll try," I said, a bit worried in case he was overrating me.

"Good! You live near?"

"Just down Riverside Road, number 135."

"Ohhh yah, Riverside. This one?" He waved his hand towards the pavement.

"Yeah. And you . . . live here?" I pointed at the rusty shack.

"Yah. It's good to watch a football ace like you, Teenage

Dladla number two in action!" He did his whistly laugh again.

I had to chuckle at him calling me an ace. Wouldn't mind if I could play like Teenage Dladla!

"Well, I'd better be going, I reckon. I've got a whole pile of homework and stuff to do," I lied.

There wasn't much homework, but I was scared that any moment I'd say something stupid and he'd realise I was actually quite a wally.

"Yah, *mnumzana*, it's good to meet you."

"Yeah, same."

"Tomorrow I must get the field ready. You play tomorrow?"

"Yeah. Maybe just as a sub."

"Good man! I'll be here to see you. Beat them one time!"

"Thanks." I felt a bit nervous in case I didn't get a chance to play after telling him I would. Also, I didn't want to make a real mess of things in front of him after he'd reckoned that I was quite good. "See you tomorrow then."

"Yah, go well, and good luck my friend!"

"Thanks."

I took off down the road with fizz in my head and springs in my feet, and Mom was all blown out of her shoes with excitement when I said they'd put me in the team. I didn't think it was such great shakes. Most of the blokes were pretty useless anyway, but it was good to see her smiling for a change.

She'd been so worried about things ever since we got to Cape Town, it was quite rare to see her looking chirpy. I reckon a lot of it must have been worry about handling things without Dad. It wasn't easy. Especially not for her. I couldn't manage all that well without him myself. I never said anything though, in case it made everyone sad again. So I reckon Mom was probably the same. Trying not to say how she felt, in case we all just felt like surrendering.

If Dad had been there, I wouldn't have lied about the bunch of lenses at school. I'd have told him they were teasing me just because Phocho was a Zulu, and not letting me play soccer and stingers and stuff, and he would have known how to sort them out. He always had the answers to that sort of thing. And I bet there must have been stacks of things Mom would have liked to ask him about too.

I must say she did a pretty good job of hiding all the strain she felt. I reckon Jenny couldn't have had any idea about it. And I only sort of noticed from seeing how she acted when she was alone, and how she was after Jenny's bedtime.

So it was really good to see her happy again.

Then I remembered her bunking work that afternoon. I said, "What were you doing hooting at me at school and making me feel a total cabbage in front of all the blokes this afternoon?"

"Oh, I had an appointment with your teacher, Mr Laing. Nice man . . ."

"What?" I was horrified. The last thing I needed was for them to find out about that one.

"Just to meet him and hear how you are getting on, nothing to worry about."

"And?"

"Well, he felt that you were fitting in well, and managing the work without any problems."

"Oh." I began to feel slightly relieved. So he hadn't said I was a wally or an idiot or anything.

"He didn't know that they called you 'Pig'. He said that was news to him and that he would never have allowed it if he'd known."

I was stunned. The men inside my head reeled round in shock. So Mom had really gone and blown it.

"You didn't tell him?" I asked in disbelief.

"Of course I did, why shouldn't I? You don't want people calling you a pig, do you?"

That was the end. I just knew it.

"Aw no, Mom. Why can't you warn me when you're going to do these things, so I can find a new school to go to before you go and blow it?"

She looked at me irritably. I suppose she couldn't understand why I was cheesed off with her for interfering in my affairs.

"Don't be silly. There's nothing wrong with talking to your teacher."

"But what if all the blokes find out that you've been to see him?"

"Don't be ridiculous, the teacher meets everyone's parents from time to time, so stop worrying. He said you were doing fine, and I was very pleased to hear it."

She might have been pleased, but I certainly wasn't.

So that was mistake number three. And it really came to the surface the next day.

Tuesday. The day of my first match. And also the day Mr Laing blew me off the map by making it look as if I went running to him about being called Pig.

He kept the class in during break and let me go, then slanged them off for about ten minutes for calling me Pig, ending off with a warning that he'd just about hang anyone who called me that again. When they were eventually released, they gushed out of the classroom and flooded towards me, all shouting and raving at once, most of them imitating baby voices and pulling childish faces at me.

"Mommy, the nasty boys at school are calling me Pig," they aped, and, "I'm a little *kaffir-boetie*." Others went on about being kept in all break for nothing because they'd never called me Pig in the first place, and that they'd get me for it.

The girls were really cheesed off because they had to stay in too, even though they had nothing to do with the whole thing.

"I didn't say that," I protested, but was shot down by a torrent of vicious threats and curses. "You can call me pig," I argued desperately, "they're more intelligent than you lot, anyway."

"Eh?" said Leon, getting all offended and shoving me backwards.

I stumbled a bit, then got my footing and stood up to him. We circled like two scorpions with their claws out, ready to rumble. My eyes were blurred from nervousness and probably also from nearly wanting to howl like a weed, but they couldn't tell. I knew I could flatten Leon as long as the others didn't go for me as well. But I had a feeling that they just might.

"Leave him," said a voice. It was Francis.

"Yeah, Leon," Andy added, "He's such a baby, he'll run to his mommy if you hit him."

Then Trevor said, "He's a *kaffir-boetie*. If you touch him you might turn black," and everyone exploded into hoots of laughter.

They turned away and left me near the cricket nets where they'd found me, feeling all shaky and alone. I wanted to go home right then and forget about the soccer match, but I couldn't. Johannes would be there to watch, and he'd think I'd been dropped from the team.

I saw Peter Green nearby. They pushed him around quite a lot too, but he was more interested in computers and things and liked being on his own, so it didn't bother him too much. At least they let him play soccer now and again. He never picked on me, so I considered going to talk to him, but he was a real weed with sulphur breath who wasn't really interested in me either, so I decided not to bother.

I held out till the afternoon without saying another word to anyone. Not even Francis, although I sat right next to him the whole day.

At the field, while we waited for the visiting team to pitch up, Mr Laing let Trevor choose which players he wanted to start with, because he was the captain. So I was left out, of course, and would only come on for the second half. In a stupid way I didn't mind at all, because it gave me less time to make mistakes in front of Johannes.

It had just occurred to me that he was supposed to be

watching. I looked round for him, and sure enough, he was sitting on the bank, just beyond the far corner from where we were, his white beard hanging over the same old frayed clothes as always. He seemed to be able to appear and disappear without being noticed. One minute he'd be there, and the next he'd be gone.

He saw me looking, and nodded his head very slightly in a kind a secret acknowledgement. I did the same back, but my head felt sort of stiff when I did it.

The visiting team arrived in a larney minibus with their school badge on it, and their coach wore a tracksuit as if he was going to play too.

Suddenly I was frightened. They looked so good, in dark blue jerseys and bright gold shorts with matching socks. We played in our ordinary old grey school socks and normal white Boxer shorts. Some of our jerseys were old and faded, and others were much too big. Maurice's totally hid his shorts when it was untucked. These blokes looked like complete pros by comparison, and then I understood what Francis had meant, and why our lot had lost every game so far.

The captains and coaches shook hands, Mr Laing tossed the coin, and the players spread out onto the field, ready to start the game.

I sat tightly on the bench with my hands wrapped round the toes of my boots, glad that I could watch for a bit before going on.

The whistle blew, and almost immediately the blue-and-golds were on the attack. Their wing took a shot that Maurice just managed to get a hand to and push for a corner. Their coach charged down the touchline, shouting orders to the players as if the game was really serious business. No wonder he needed a tracksuit.

As they prepared for the corner kick, I could see Johannes beyond the action. He was nodding to me gravely.

There was a goalmouth scramble that had their coach screaming for action and just about having a frothy on the spot, but we eventually managed to clear the ball. The game went on for a few minutes with them in our half just about the whole time, but not managing to score, which didn't do much good for their coach's heart condition, I shouldn't think. Then suddenly, without warning, Benjy and Trevor broke away against the run of play and scored.

Their coach was blown out of his underpants. His mouth just hung open, silent for a change. Our lot couldn't believe it either.

Mr Laing blew the whistle, a bit louder than usual I reckon, then they restarted.

The Boughton coach didn't have to worry about having a heart attack though, because they soon scored the equaliser. Then a few minutes later they scored again. And again. And then a fourth goal just before the half-time had me feeling pretty sorry for Maurice. He must have felt a complete lens, letting in four goals in one half! Every time Boughton scored, our blokes would blame him as if it was all his fault. Meanwhile it was everyone's fault for letting them get so many chances to shoot.

Each goal they scored had been making me more nervous, but by the half-time whistle I didn't worry any more. The game was such a walkover anyway. I could hardly do much worse.

Mr Laing gave Terry a rest for the second half, so I took his damp jersey to replace him in defence.

The game restarted, and I must have been about the third bloke to touch the ball as they surged forward again, this time attacking the goal at the river end. I intercepted a long pass, dodged a player, and sent the ball upfield to Richard. I noticed that Johannes had moved round to the river end at half-time to watch where most of the action would probably be. That didn't make me feel any more comfortable, but after my first touch of the ball I became a lot less shaky and started to feel more normal.

We managed to keep them away from Maurice for about five minutes, but eventually they had to break through and their centre forward sent a ripping shot into the corner that Maurice could never have reached. It was his hat trick, so all the players jumped on him and shook his hand and hugged him, carrying on like a bunch of idiots who must have thought he'd turned into a girl or something, just because he scored three goals. It was pathetic.

After what seemed like about an hour of grisly battle, the final whistle went. We'd lost five-one. I suppose it could have been worse when you look at what the score was at half time.

"Three cheers for the ref," their hat trick hero captain shouted, "Hibbip, ray, hibbip, ray, hibbip, ray," and then, "Three cheers for Chelsea Road!"

They were pretty half-hearted cheers, but not half as bad as ours were for them.

We each shook hands with the nearest few players and said things that we didn't mean, like "Well played," and "Thanks for the game," and as suddenly as they'd arrived, they were gone.

So was Johannes. I reckoned he couldn't have been too impressed with his new ace player.

No one felt like saying much, and two lighties who'd been watching even managed to kick the ball around because the main ous were feeling too miserable to bother. I collected my gear and headed off home without saying a word.

As I passed the stream end of the ground I heard, "Fsst!"

I smiled.

Chapter 6

The party

Johannes reckoned I'd played a real steamer of a game. He said if I hadn't come on in the second half, the other team would've scored eight goals.

I must say I hadn't thought of it like that. It made me feel like a mountain, although I knew it wasn't totally true. It was a good thing I hadn't been on in the first half, otherwise he couldn't have said that.

We had two tins' worth of tea and a long talk next to the fire that afternoon, mainly I suppose because he said, "*Hawu!* They must be pleased with you," and I said they weren't, and told him why.

He took off about how lousy blokes can be to new people, like when he couldn't speak Zulu when he first got to Durban, and that they must be jealous, and all about nicknames and teachers and how they can actually help, and that I shouldn't blame Mom because she was only doing what she thought was best, and all sorts of other things.

So then I changed my mind about the Phocho thing and decided to tell him how they picked on me just because my best friend was a Zulu. I hadn't had the guts to mention it before, but suddenly it seemed right, so I did.

I expected him to really explode about that, but he didn't. I couldn't believe it. It was as if he already knew and understood the whole thing. It must have made him a bit sad to know that about the soccer team that played on his ground though, but he just told me not to give up on them. Reckoned I should prove to them that I was a worthwhile friend even if they weren't, and keep trying to join in with whatever they did until they finally got tired of stopping me. He thought I should show them I was capable of being friends with everyone. That Zulu and Xhosa people were just like anyone else.

It began to drizzle as we spoke, the fine dots hissing in the fire, and behind us wet frogs creeched like rusty hinges. So we moved inside, into his tiny shack, dark and close with a steel bedstead raised on bricks. Everything smelt of fire, such a strong race back to Greytown, it took me quite by surprise. And from then on I loved his little room. It was as if part of Phocho's old compound had been captured in there.

Johannes hoisted himself aboard his bed like the captain of a ship and shnicked on a transistor radio with a wire hanger for an aerial. He clicked his fingers to the happy *mbaqanga* rhythm crackling through with saxophones and things. I sat on the chair at a rickety table, cupping my hands round the hot mug, smiling.

It all made so much sense when he said things. I wondered why I hadn't realised what he'd told me all along, and decided it was because I never talked to anyone. You only realise things when you say them to somebody, and I didn't have Phocho to talk to any more. Or Dad.

Even though I'd had a really stinking day at school, he had me walking on balloons by the time I left him, and all keen to try out the things he'd suggested.

I didn't tell Mom about the disaster she'd caused. I was planning to, but Johannes made me feel so guilty about it that I changed my mind. I said I'd had a good day. Told her how I just about single-handedly staved off a humiliating defeat at soccer. I explained that five-one was only an embarrassing defeat, and that eight-one was a humiliating defeat, but somehow it didn't sound as convincing as when Johannes had said it.

Next day they still wouldn't let me play soccer in their childish netball field game.

They told me to play with kaffirs or go feeding pigs and that I wasn't Goodenough for them, and all sorts of other pathetically tired comments. I tried to tell them that Zulus were no different from them, except maybe friendlier, which nearly got me into one hell of a fight. Then they challenged me to go and tell Mr Laing that they'd been calling me Pig again, knowing full well that I couldn't because I'd said they could call me anything they wanted to.

So the name stayed with me like a burr stuck in my underrods wherever I went. The only time they didn't use it was when Mr Laing was around. Then they didn't call me anything at all.

Only Johannes called me Mike. When he wasn't calling me *mnumzana*, that is.

The teachers, Mom and Jenny all called me Michael, which I reckon is a pretty naffish name, to tell the truth.

The girls weren't too bad I suppose, but that's only comparing them with the blokes. They never spoke to me either, not that I particularly had anything to say to them — one sister is more than enough girls to have around — but at least they weren't out to pull a sly one on me like the blokes were. Stella and Carol were definitely the ring leaders on the female front, organising just about everything the girls did. They also left the naffs out of everything, just like Trevor and Mally did. (Not that I think I was a naff, but Peter Green definitely was.) Plenty of the girls were naffs, so they could do their own thing when they got left out.

It was a lot harder for me. I could either do things with Sulphuric Peter or hang around with the lighties, and seeing that it was such a good choice, I didn't bother to do either.

Most days on the way home from school I stopped for tea and told Johannes how things were getting on, or rather how they weren't. I always had the chipped mug, he chose the big jam tin, and we drank great volumes of smoky tea beside the fire, just talking. He'd keep giving me hope and new things to try whenever I felt like giving up. But apart from him, I don't reckon I had any friends to talk to, really.

Nearly two weeks had passed since my first soccer match. I hadn't been picked for the following game, and I'd just been left out again. It was already June. We were nearly half-way through the season and I'd only played one game, so things weren't going too well for me on that gloomy Monday. But Johannes never seemed to give up. Always trying his best to make me look on the bright side. So when I told him about a party the girls were planning, he just about bounced me off my rock, he was so excited.

"Yah good, man!" he shouted. "A party, Mike! A party! Just right!"

"Why?"

"You say the girls aren't bad to you?"

I wasn't so sure, but I was keen to hear his idea. "Yeah?"

"Well, you get *them* to invite you." He clasped his hands together with a loud, satisfied clap.

I looked a bit worried.

"Well, what's wrong?"

"I'm not so sure they'll let me come along."

"Who, the mamas?"

"What?"

"You worry the ladies don't have you at their party?"

"Yeah . . ."

"You must be mad. *Med*!" He tapped his temples with a laugh. "You know why they not bad to you?"

"No?"

"Because they *love* you, Mike, that's why." He cackled merrily and I sat watching him uncertainly. I reckoned maybe it was worth a try.

"Okay, I'll see if I can get invited," I said after a deep breath.

"Yah, *mnumzana*. Good man! I don't want to speak to you tomorrow if you don't go, eh? No more sad boy!"

"Okay."

Somehow Johannes never seemed to give up, even though he had nothing going for himself. I mean, when you're about sixty-five or whatever, and little white school kids still laugh and call you a coon boy, when the hell do you become a man?

It wasn't long before I got a chance to start greasing for an invitation. Next morning the girls were getting all excited about Friday night, chirping over who was going to bring what records, and who would be with this ou and that guy and things, so I decided to act thick about the whole thing and ask them what was up.

It wasn't as easy as it might sound, plucking up the guts to just go up to them and ask. I'd never really talked to them before, so I was more than just chicken. I suppose you could say I was ostrich. That's how scared I was.

I watched them sort of sideways as they squeaked and raved about the whole show. No blokes were unpacking in the classroom, so at least they wouldn't see me making a chop of myself. But I had to move fast before it was too late.

"Right, this is it," I said to myself, taking a deep breath and hoping they wouldn't hear the thumping from my chest. I moved towards them.

Just then Trevor burst through the door, slung his bag down and started pulling socks and rotten sarmies out. As he appeared, I did an immediate about-turn and pretended to tidy my desk. He took ages to sort his stupid junk out, and by the time he'd finished, Neil, Richard, Alexander, Mally and about a hundred others had poured into the room. They all started talking to the girls about the useless party, so I left in disgust, kicking myself for not acting sooner.

But my luck soon changed once I got outside. Stella was hanging around the quad on her own. So, before I could chicken out again, I strode up to her rather stiffly, and with a pounding heart and tacky mouth asked, "Are you going to a party on Friday night?" I felt a cabbage as soon as I said it because it was a really thick quesiton.

She was so startled at me speaking to her that she spun round to see if I was talking to someone behind her.

She looked back again with wide eyes and said, "No."

I knew that was a stinking lie, but then she continued: "I'm not going to one, I'm *having* one, you cretin."

I wondered what a cretin was, hoping she didn't realise that I didn't know. "You mean it's at your place?" (Another ridiculous question.)

"Yeah."

"Who's going?"

"Lotsa people. Why?"

"Well . . ." I felt my face going red-hot as I stammered, "I just wondered . . . I . . . um . . ."

"You wanna come?" She sounded almost sarcastic, as if she couldn't believe her own words.

I nearly chickened out on the spot, but then I remembered Johannes.

"Yes," I said boldly, then crumbled. "If . . . I'm allowed to . . .?"

She gave a huge, I-can't-believe-this type of sigh, looked through the top of her head, tightened her lips and blinked snottily. I felt like dying. I wished I hadn't been such a wally as to have asked her in the first place. It was so obvious she hated me just as much as the blokes did. I should have known better, seeing that she was Trevor's favourite.

"I *s'pose* so," she said reluctantly.

I wasn't sure I'd heard right.

"Really?!" I nearly jumped out from beneath my hairstyle.

"If you *have* to."

She wasn't keen, that's for sure, but she'd said yes, and that was all that counted.

"*Thanks!*"

I ran off even faster than my drumming heart. Things were happening!

"You've done it!" I said aloud, then quickly looked round in case someone had heard me.

Stella went off to the classroom, so I sneaked round to the windows to listen out for anything interesting. As I got there,

I heard Trevor say, "Aw no you didn't?" There was an assortment of incredulous noises and comments, so I knew that she'd told them. Now there was nothing they could do.

Johannes was so pleased when I told him, anyone would think he was the one who wanted to go to the party.

Every time I thought about it, I got more and more nervous. I'd probably make a real lens of myself because I'd never danced before. They were bound to spend the whole night bouncing and leaping around, and if I didn't join in, they'd think I was a total wet. So suddenly I found myself wishing I hadn't listened to Johannes, mainly because I was a bit of a coward at heart. Mom thought it was bloody marvellous of course. She carried on more or less like Johannes did, as if it was her party or something.

"I want to go too," Jenny whined.

I felt like telling them all to go instead of me, seeing that they were so much keener than I was about the whole thing.

"Don't be silly," Mom said, "Michael's friends are much too old for you."

Friends! I liked that one. I didn't have the guts to admit that I'd had to ask for the invitation.

"We'll have to get some new clothes for you," Mom reckoned, "We can't have you looking shabby for the party." She thought the whole thing was pretty serious stuff.

"No, no," I objected nervously.

"Oh, stop being silly now. We can't have your friends thinking you come from a refugee camp. I'll have a look for some nice trousers for you at lunch-time tomorrow. Just about everyone in town's having a sale at the moment."

She was really taking over.

The next evening she arrived with a completely naffish pair of rods for me to try.

When I complained about them, she said, "Oh, don't be ridiculous, everyone's wearing them," and, "They fit you fine."

So there I was, trapped into going to a party in a pair of rods that made me look like a clown. I thought of running

75

away to get out of it. Or pretending to be sick on Friday afternoon. But I was useless at conning Mom about being sick. She knew me far too well for me to pull off that stunt. After a few minutes of desperate thinking, I resigned myself to the fact that if I wasn't dead by Friday, I'd have to go. And the chances were I wouldn't be, seeing that I'd already lived more than a decade without snuffing it.

"Where is it?" Mom asked.

"Eh?"

"Where's the party?"

A gong rang in my head. I hadn't found that out.

"Er, at Stella's place. I'm still going to get the address."

I didn't even need to ask for the address the next day. First thing after putting my stuff down, Stella, Carol, Trevor and Mally came up to me all rowdy and quizzy to ask if I knew where her place was.

"No, I was gonna ask today."

Mally turned to Carol and said, "See, I told you . . ."

"Shut up!" Stella snapped. "We thought you didn't know, so I've drawn a map for you."

She held out a page torn from an exercise book. There was a crabby-looking map on it with crossings out, scribbles and corrections. I couldn't believe how decent they were being to me. Johannes had been right about the party being the way to get through to them. It was amazing.

"Thanks." I cleared my throat to give myself time to think what to say, but my head was empty, so I just said, "Thanks a lot."

I was actually smiling. So was Mally, even though I was convinced he was out to expire my meter.

"Pleasure," said Carol, and they ran off as suddenly as they'd appeared.

I must have been quite excited about the party, I reckon, because I even showed the map to Jenny after school, as if to say, "Look, here's proof that I've been invited to the party." I'd have shown it to Johannes too if he'd been at his spot on the way home, but he must have had the afternoon off. In fact, he must have had a couple of days off because I didn't see him on the Friday either.

That afternoon I started to get a bit shaky each time I thought about the party. The fairies wouldn't stop dancing in my stomach. I wished I was as good at it as them.

Mom came home with a really larney shirt for me. It was a huge improvement on the clown rods, but together they still made me look like a total cabbage. Anyway, I felt sorry for her because she tried so hard to do the right things for us, so I said I'd changed my mind about the naff rods and that I liked them too, and that the shirt and rods went together perfectly.

Then she started trying to brush a side parting in my hair, so I had to put my foot down. You've got to draw the line somewhere with moms, and that was it. As soon as she'd finished sandpapering my scalp with the brush, I mussed my hair up in the mirror again.

"What are you doing?" she asked, horrified that I should be so disrespectful of her hairdressing expertise.

"It's the fashion."

"Nonsense!"

"Well, its *my* fashion."

She shrugged and surrendered. I wasn't going to have to have a naff's hairstyle as well.

By the end of supper Jenny had successfully whined her way into coming for the ride in the car. The last thing I needed was to be spotted arriving at the party in the old rattletrap, complete with mother and baby sister. So I extracted a promise from them that they'd drop me on the corner and let me walk the last stretch. Mom started muttering, so I said I wasn't going unless she agreed to my terms of the contract. She could see I was serious about it and gave in, but made it clear she thought I was being "very silly". "Strategic" was what I called it.

It was quite a relief after a few roads to discover that the map made sense. I'd half expected it to have false names and things to make me look a real chop. And luckily it was dark when they dropped me off, so the chances of being seen were considerably reduced. They drove off, waving to me and calling out excruciating goodbyes which I was convinced Trevor would hear, wherever he was.

I took off down the party road lined with low-flying trees. Each time I passed one, I jumped to grab at the leaves. The more I managed to catch, the luckier I would be at the party.

Number 37 went past on a rusted old letter-box that used to be yellow. I wanted 49. Gradually my heart started kicking about its cage (its usual trick) as the dreaded house got nearer. I looked down at my clown rods. They weren't as bad as I'd originally thought. Maybe because I couldn't see the colour properly in the streetlighting.

The gate loomed ahead. It stared at me with a white plastic 49 on it. Each numeral had two black eyes from the rusted screws. I froze for a moment. Lights were on in the house, but the noise hadn't started. I unlatched the gate and cringed as it squeaked at the top of its voice. I hate gates that give you away. For a moment I was tempted to turn and flee. But then I thought I'd probably run smack into Trevor and Mally or someone. That would be a big laugh for them. "We caught Pig chickening out of the party, ha ha." I could just hear it.

The sound of a TV carried from the lounge. My heart was busy trying to pound itself loose from its mountings, so I knocked quickly before I had a seizure, then waited in the swirling darkness for about six days before the shuffling feet arrived at the door. It opened and a fossil with thin glasses squinted at me.

"Yes?" Her "s" whistled loudly.

"Um," suddenly I realised something was horribly wrong, "Have I come to the right house for the party?"

"Party?" The old bag looked totally confused. And I realised I'd been tricked.

"Um, I'm looking for Stella's house."

"Stella? Stella who?" She must have though I was mad.

"Pugin."

"No, dear, you've got the wrong house," she whistled her "s" again. "Maybe you want the folks across the road. They have lots of kids round at the weekend."

I realised it was no use, so I made a quick excuse: "Wait a minute. I'm supposed to be at 39, not 49, I've just remembered. Sorry about that."

"Oh. Never mind, dear. I hope you find them."

"I will."

"Enjoy yourself."

I escaped onto the pavement and stood for a long time, feeling slightly sick. What was the next move supposed to be in a spot like that? I couldn't let Mom and Jenny know I'd been tricked, so I couldn't phone them to fetch me. I just wanted to collapse and pack it in with life, there and then.

So much for all the good luck leaves I'd jumped for.

At first I pondered on what to do to Trevor and the rest of the scummy bogeyheads who thought it was a big joke to send me off on a wild goose chase, then I realised I'd be playing right into their hands if I let them know their trick had worked. So I decided to pretend I'd had something more important on and didn't bother to take up their invitation. That way I could enjoy the look on their faces. The thought gave me the strength to set off for home. I'd need it. It had taken long enough to get there by car.

At the end of the road I turned right, the way we'd come, and retraced our route for a few turns until I got to an intersection that had me totally stumped. We could have come from any one of three roads. I just couldn't remember.

It was almost time for panic stations when I thought of the map. I slapped at my clown rods pockets and heard a reassuring crackle. It was still there. The very thing that was used to trick me had suddenly become my means of survival. Maybe the luck of the leaves had worked after all.

It took me about an hour and a half to get home.

Of course Mom wanted to know why I'd come back on my

own so early instead of waiting for her, but I was ready for that. I'd had plenty of time to work my story out. I made up some lie about being able to get an early lift with Maurice. Saved her the trouble of having to come out and fetch me.

"Oh, you didn't need to worry," she said.

Oh yes I did.

Chapter 7

To the river

Their faces on Monday were worth every bit of my walk home. They kept coming up to me in ones and twos with barely disguised laughs to ask me why I didn't come to the party, expecting me to tell them I couldn't find it or something. And their disappointment was glorious as I told them I'd gone instead to a huge do with a live band that went on past midnight.

"Oh yeah?" Mally reckoned, all sceptical, "and who's party was it?"

But I'd thought it all out and said, "It was a giant reunion party only for people with hunting, horse-riding and farming experience."

Mally looked stunned, and in the background I noticed that Andy was listening in. I was enjoying what was probably my finest moment since arriving at the school. So I went on, making sure to let them know that none of them would ever have qualified for this really amazing party.

"And you were only allowed to come if you'd caught a bass bigger than *this*." With my hands I indicated the size of the biggest bass I'd ever caught. Actually, to be totally accurate, it was about twice the size of my biggest one, but they weren't to know.

Mally was struck dumb.

Andy decided to stop pretending he wasn't listening: "How did you get invited?"

"The Mayor."

"What!" He was astonished. So was I. It just came out automatically. I couldn't believe how smoothly I was lying.

It didn't bother me though, they deserved to be lied to after the dirty trick they'd played on me.

"The Mayor of Cape Town knows our family personally, and he happened to know that I've shot with a 4.10 and twelve bore shotgun as well as a .22." I was really cooking. "And he read in the papers about the junior bass fishing record I broke in Greytown, so I was a kind of guest of honour . . ."

"Jeez!" Andy was totally taken in.

Mally turned away in disgust. He couldn't stand hearing any more, so he slunk off to find the others.

Outside I found the gang hanging around at the tennis court, not playing stingers or anything. Just standing around. And they all shut up as soon as I appeared. What a giveaway. I knew they'd been talking about me, but for once I didn't mind. Mally and Andy had obviously told them all how important I was. It almost made me feel guilty!

"So I hear you're quite the main ou?" said Trevor, kind of taking up the challenge.

"No," I said modestly, pretending to be James Bond or someone.

"Well, that's not what I hear. Apparently you're the big-time hunter and fisherman? I suppose you're extra special for hanging around with kaffirs as well. Well that's quite funny isn't it? I mean, how come you're such a main ou and yet you've got to get your mommy," at this stage, his scathing tone changed to a feeble sort of put-on baby's voice, "to fight your battles for you?"

"I didn't . . ."

"Oh no? Well what about 'Mommy they call me Pig, and if they don't stop I'm gonna cry?' and, 'Sir, look at Trevor, he hasn't done his project'?"

"I never told anyone."

The whole gang chorused boos at me.

"I told you, you can call me Pig, I don't mind. They're far better animals than some others I could name." I said it looking straight at Trevor.

"Eh?"

"Pigs. I like them. You can call me what you like — it doesn't bother me. An' if you say kaffir again, I'll bloody flatten you!"

"What?" For a moment Trevor was paralysed by the sudden shock of my threat, then he recovered and came towards me. "What did you just say?"

"Come on Trevor," Francis grabbed him by the sleeve.

Trevor shook himself free and stood two inches from my face for a horribly long time.

"Come on Trevor, leave him," Francis urged. "Let's go."

Reluctantly he turned and they all moved off.

I must say I felt a bit relieved because I didn't feel up to rumbling with Trevor. I reckon he would have flattened me, more like. Mally was probably more my league.

Later on I just couldn't sit still in class. Somehow, even though they'd had a go at me, it was my round, the first time I'd actually managed to hold my own, and I felt pretty good about it too. The problem was, the better I did against them, the more they wanted to get me, as I soon found out.

That afternoon at soccer Mr Laing put me on the wing next to Richard and Francis. We were in the red team. Mally and Trevor were in the blues. Richard was at least decent enought to pass to me when I was in a good position, unlike Trevor and Mally, who'd do anything to keep the ball rather than give me a chance.

I'd missed the team's last two matches, mainly because Mr Laing never got to see whether I could play or not, but finally I felt my chance had arrived. And I was right. My luck of the morning hadn't run out. I played a steamer of a game, scoring twice as we beat the blues three-one.

Mr Laing was so impressed, he picked me to play right wing in Tuesday's match. From the corner of my eye I noticed Mally make a move to protest, then change his mind.

"Mally, we'll put you at right half for the time being."

"But sir . . ."

"Do you want to play?"

"Sir."

"Well, then you'll play where I put you. Understood?"

"Sir."

As soon as Mr Laing's back was turned, Mally raised his fist to me and mouthed, "I'll get you!"

I could feel that trouble was brewing. The air was electric with it. Trevor had been itching to get his hands on me after I'd opened by big gob and said I'd flatten him, Mally was ready for war, and I could tell that the others had picked up the vibe. Like sharks detecting blood in the water.

I wasn't planning on being some struggling fish waiting to get eaten, so at the end of practice I pretended nothing was wrong, but got my things together as quickly as possible. I wanted to get out of there before Mr Laing left, but he was in his jalopy and gone before I could. I couldn't run, because that would have been a giveaway, so I just started walking off pretty smartly, my ears tense and my hair prickling. I couldn't see them, but I knew they were turning on me even before Trevor opened his mouth.

"Hey you ous!" he shouted. "It's time to christen our new kaffir player! Pig *Mkhize*-not-so-Goodenough!"

Andy whooped like a crazed warrior and everyone packed onto me.

"You've got to be christened before you can be a regular member of the team," Trevor said. "We've all been through this." Then he tipped his face up to the sky and yelled, *"To the riverrrr!"* with gob boiling in the back of his throat.

"Yeeeehaa!" they shouted as they carried me across the field, pulling my boots and socks off, throwing them as far as they could. I saw one bouncing off the goal post, chased by three struggling players, each trying to kick it into the net before the others. Heads and flailing arms were in the way, so I couldn't see where my other stuff went. Someone was rubbing mud or something into my hair.

"It's dog shit!" yelled a voice, and there was another chorus of whoops.

"*Kaffir-boeties* get extra special treatment!"

I heard running water between the war cries, then Trevor's voice above the others, organising the operation. "Watch out . . . mind the water. We don't want to get *ourselves* wet and muddy now, just this dirty pig here!"

"Yeah! Scrub the kaffir stink off him!"

Screeches of wild laughter followed.

I kicked and struggled, but the arms tightened their grip. There must have been about ten of them holding me. My head got dangerously close to the water as they slipped and stumbled on the banks of the stream. Then they braced themselves to drop me. "Okay ous, are you ready?" yelled Trevor. "One . . . two . . . threeee!"

The razor-coldness shocked my breath away. A rock stabbed into my shoulder, and before I could recover, boots clamped over my chest. A big black set of studs covered my choking face, jabbing into my forehead, pushing me down until the icy flood gurgled over my eyes. I had to have air, but the gouging foot trapped my face underwater. I couldn't see. Mad hands pulled at my feet, and then I panicked. I was going to wet my pants, I could feel it. Then they would laugh, but it didn't matter.

I was dying. They were drowning me. My mouth took a frantic gulp of freezing slime, making me kick in desperation.

Someone splashed into the river, then I heard a voice some miles away say, "Okay Mally, that's enough now."

The boot lifted off my face, and Mally stood back as I sat in the current coughing water and snot, trying to breathe.

Something hit me on the back of the head, I reckon it was a boot. Then Mally kicked at my ribs before they dragged me out and tripped me onto the mud. Hands cupped over the back of my head and ground my face into the stinking muck. Like Phocho's shoe. But this time it wasn't funny.

They obviously thought it was, judging by the way they laughed.

They scrummed on top of me with their studs tearing into my body, then booted me till I crumpled up and cried.

"Leave me! Leave me!" I wailed from the ground, covering my head from the kicks. Between sniffs I heard their jeering voices, but I kept my eyes closed.

"Pig's a little naff. He can't take it."

"Baby."

"He's not a pig, he's a piglet!" Peals of laughter.

"I suppose you're going to tell mommy you couldn't take it, eh, little cry baby?"

"Naff!"

I didn't say anything. I just lay there.

"Well, I'll tell you something," it was Trevor's voice. "If you tell anyone about this, you little *kaffir-boetie*, we'll have to do it to you all over again, won't we guys?" There was a big cheer, even from the Standard Fours, who felt they could, now that they'd seen me crying. "And you *won't* come to soccer practice again. We'll see to that, eh ous?" Another cheer.

"Bye baby piggy."

They moved off and left me on the ground, shivering. It wasn't from the cold either. I was too numb and sore to feel the cold. It was what they'd done to me that made me shiver.

Once they'd gone I got up, fighting the tears, with spears ripping pain in my legs and shoulder, and started looking for my boots and socks. They were in a total mess, like the rest of me, but not too badly damaged, so I put them on and limped across the field, hoping to get home and clean up before anyone noticed the state I was in.

"*Hawu!* Mike, what happened?" The voice from the bushes took me by surprise.

I'd almost forgotten Johannes, he'd been away for so long. His eyes were on stalks as he goggled at me, the mess I must have looked. His mouth hung open like a real cartoon character.

"I got christened," I said and tried to laugh, but it turned into a cry.

"*Hawu, hawu, hawu*, sorry man. Don't cry, *mnumzana*. Who did this to you?"

"Everyone."

I sobbed like a baby, feeling really sorry for myself.

He clicked his tongue and swore in Xhosa, looking round with a fiery face as if he was about to get up and go after them. "Why, why, why?"

"To make me part of the team."

"*Hawu ayibo!*" He shook his head in disbelief.

I couldn't stop acting like a baby. Somehow, when someone felt pity for me, it made me want to cry even more.

"Easy, eeasy, boy," he said, putting a big arm round me and holding me as I quietened down. He smelt of fire, like home. Greytown home. "You tell the teacher what these *skelems* do, Mike. He'll fix them good for you."

"I can't."

"Why?" He was horrified, "*Hawu!* Why not man?"

"Because they said they'll do it again if I do."

"Never!" he roared, his voice quivering with rage, "Never!" He swore again in Xhosa. His great, blurred fist clenched and unclenched next to my cheek as he spoke. "They'll never do that. If the teacher knows, he helps you. They won't *dare* to do it. I whip them if they ever *touch* you again. I whip them, even if your teacher don't."

"Yeah," I sniffed, "yeah, I suppose so."

But inside I knew I wasn't going to tell anyone. It was the naff's way out, and even though I'd cried, I knew I wasn't really a naff. Dad always said a bloke should fight his own battles, and I reckon he was right, judging by the mess Mom made of the Pig episode.

Johannes raved on about what animals they were to treat a "good *mnumzana*" like me the way they did, and that they weren't fit to live in a pigsty, never mind go round calling people pigs. Then he stopped when he realised how much I was shivering.

"You get home, *mnumzana*, get dry, before you catch a *bed* cold."

I enjoyed the silly way he always called me *mnumzana*, sort of as if I was a man or something.

His face turned serious. Thinking for a while. Then he spoke slowly, very slowly, with a faraway look in his eyes: "Yah . . . it's very bad . . . sitting in wet clothes . . ." Then he came back to earth. "You get dry." He gave me a hard squeeze, then pushed me away. "Go now. From now, you don't take no . . . shit from those *skelems*. No more! Right Mike?"

"Right."

It really made him sound cross when he swore in English. It was so sort of unnatural, I suppose.

"Good, man. Go well, my friend."

He really knew how to convert me back into a human being again. I reckon he couldn't have realised what a lifesaver he was.

At home I crept through the hedge into the garden, hoping Jenny would be at a friend's place. The last thing I needed was for her to find out what had happened and go and blow the whole thing again. But I was out of luck. There were voices coming from her bedroom. She would see n e as I went down the passage to my room or the bathroom, but I had to clean myself up a bit before Mom got home.

I stood in the back garden trying to puzzle that one out for a while when a gust of sub-zero wind bit into my arms and sent me straight to my window. It's mad how the torture of the cold just suddenly gets you going. I suppose something inside you says, "Listen, do you want to die, or are you going to do something?"

I'd often wondered if I could fit through the middle of our burglar guards, and I was about to find out. They had a kind of an "s" pattern, and in the middle there were two of these "s" things facing each other, leaving a heart-shaped hole that could possibly be climbed through. Grabbing two of the bars, I launched myself up onto the sloping sill and sort of wedged my backside there, scraping a muddy foot on the wall as I did so. Then I had to reach in and loosen the brass mushroom thing to open the window as wide as it could go. The frame dug into my shoulder as I stretched, stabbing a place where I'd been kicked, making me wince involuntarily. The voices next door stopped. I could sense them listening nervously for another sound, so I held on, hardly breathing for fear of getting caught.

At last the talking continued. And so did I. The window swung wide open, letting me stick my head and shoulder through the gap. As I slid halfway inside, the bar scraped a button off my shirt. I watched it tick to the floor as I hung helplessly from the grid. The talking stopped again, then footsteps approached. I was stuck. There was nothing I could do. Jenny and some other lightie appeared at the door. My face was red from hanging the wrong way up, and with difficulty I tilted it towards them.

"I thought it was you," Jenny said. "What are you doing in the window? You're all wet and muddy!"

So she had eyes. I'd always wondered. Huh! A fine mess I'd got myself into again. My mind raced. I had to come up with something that would shut her up before she told Mom.

"Yeah. I . . . ", but my mind was vacant, "I fell in the river."

"What were you doing at the river?"

"Catching crabs." Then suddenly a change of plan: "No, I was fetching the ball, actually, and I slipped in the mud an' fell in the water."

"Why're you climbing through the window?"

"I want to." That was a really feeble one. Even a lightie like Jenny would find that a bit hard to swallow, so to make it a bit more likely, I added, "I wanted to sneak in and give you a fright while I was in such a mess."

I finally managed to slide myself head first into a pile on the floor, and sat there rubbing my legs.

"Mommy's gonna be cross."

"Yeah, but don't tell her about me climbing through the window, okay?"

"What'll you give me?"

Little sisters have no mercy. They'll pounce on you when you're dying and see what they can get out of you.

I sighed, "Uh, anything." Then, realising how dangerous that could be, "a Kit Kat."

"I don't like them any more," she said with the threatening tone of someone in a good bargaining position.

"Okay, well . . . what do you like?"

"Crunchies!"

"All right, one."

"Two."

"What?"

"Two." She was unflinching, holding me to ransom.

"Okay, two, but I'll have to pay you in instalments."

"Big ones," she ordered, and with that they turned and went back to her room to carry on pulling doll's eyes out, or whatever they do for fun once they've finished bankrupting their brothers.

I ran a scorching hot bath to get rid of the shivers and the slimy stink before Mom could get home. At least I'd got the dirty clothes story worked out. Then I saw my face in the mirror and realised to my horror that I'd have to make an addition to the story: I'd have to say the black eye happened when I fell. Must have hit it on a rock or something.

Chapter 8

Secret supplies

Johannes knew what it was like to be cold and wet. I'd been able to tell from his face that he'd been there enough times himself.

I lay in bed, staring at the swirlies in the darkness, just thinking about things. All sorts of things. Like how easily I'd conned Mom into believing that it was just an accident. The clothes and the black eye. And how Dad would have known straight away that it was a sprout-story. I decided not to say a word about the christening at school, even though they'd been so lousy to me, and then they'd realise that I wasn't really a naff like they thought I was. That I was actually better than them, because I'd never do something like that to anyone. Never pick on someone just because of the type of friends they had. Maybe one day I'd tell them that I'd never sink so low, and they'd all feel pretty lousy about it. And I'd say, "Never mind, I can handle it. It's just time you learnt to behave like proper human beings towards other human beings."

Then I thought about Johannes again. I kept seeing his face, and hearing him say. "Yah . . . it's very bad . . . sitting in wet clothes . . ." It made me shudder, remembering how I'd felt in the freezing wind, wondering how to get inside. Imagine if I hadn't had a place to go to, to get dry.

I couldn't sleep. My head was full of things I wished I'd said to them while they were getting stuck into me. All sorts of things that would have made them feel ashamed of themselves, and things that would have made them stop thinking I was a naff. Then I would twist and curl awkwardly as I remembered how I'd cried in front of them. Even some of the Standard Four lighties had seen me crying. Suddenly I'd discover that my fists were tight with fury as I thought about the whole thing. Mally had a bloody cheek to tease me about Phocho. Phocho was a real friend, not a plastic weed like him. He was more worried about acting tough than being anyone's friend. One day they would realise how pathetically shallow their big gang of main ous really was. They were the types who wouldn't bother to stick up for each other when the crunch really came. I stepped up to Mally and grabbed him by the neck and strangled him. As he choked his last few breaths, I growled bitterly between clenched teeth, "I only wanted to be friends with you and the other blokes, but you wouldn't listen, so now I'm afraid you'll have to pay the price . . ."

"Please, I'll be nice to you . . ."

"It's too late for that. You've gone one step too far."

I rolled onto my back and wrestled with the blankets, pulled the pillow over my head and tried to think about nothing. But Trevor was there and I had to strangle him too. I ducked him in the swimming-pool and stood on his head until the bubbles stopped coming up and his feeble struggles died away. Then Johannes sat shivering on his rock, arms clutched around himself. "It's very bad . . . sitting in wet clothes . . ."

"Don't worry," I said, "I've brought some good, dry clothes for you."

I sat up immediately, startling my pillow to the floor. That was it! I could give Johannes some clothes. Dad's old clothes!

I spent the rest of the night thrashing around, then sleeping fitfully between moments of planning and thinking. Of course, when I finally managed to fall asleep properly it was just about time to get up.

After breakfast I hung back and waited for Mom to leave.

As the front door slammed, I charged for the ancient trunk and wrestled with the catches. Mom hadn't had the heart to get rid of Dad's old clothes, but it was silly to keep them, so I didn't mind taking a few. No one would miss them.

I'd kind of braced myself for looking at his old clothes again. I'd known it would be hard. But when I got the trunk open, the smell of his pipe shocked me badly. His special smell was still there. My voice called out. And the word that came out was "Dad!" as the waft of sweet Mellow Wood hit me. I saw Dad in front of the fire with his feet up. That time it had actually snowed. We were laughing because he'd been teasing me with words. We often used to play with words . . .

"Michael, what you doing?" Jenny called from the front door.

That knocked me back to earth. I thought she'd gone ahead.

"Nothing. I mean, I'm coming. Just wait at the door."

I listened for a second to make sure she wasn't coming down the passage, then rummaged through the clothes. I dug out a sports coat similar to the one Johannes wore, because he must have liked that sort of thing, and picked two shirts and a pair of rods that didn't look too old-fashioned, then stuffed them into my bag and forced the clips closed.

Usually Johannes was up working at the clubhouse in the mornings on the way to school, but that morning he'd hung around to see how I was.

"Jenny, you go on ahead. I'll catch up with you before the bridge."

I didn't want her to see me hauling the clothes out. It would be a definite death sentence for me if I got caught pulling off that stunt. She scowled at me.

"I won't be long. I'll catch you up before the bridge, I promise. If I don't, I'll buy you a Kit Kat . . . I mean a Crunchie."

"You already owe me two."

"Another one."

"Okay."

"But if you run, you're disqualified, okay?"

"Okay."

She took off as if she was in a walking race, hell-bent on scoring another Crunchie off me. Three in two days is pretty good going. In fact, it was too good going, so I'd have to catch her before I got myself into debt for life.

Johannes raised a hand. "How are you, *mnumzana*?"

"Okay today, and you?"

"No, good . . . good, can't complain. You got a bad eye there man, Mike."

"Yeah," I laughed.

"Is it hurting?"

"No. Not really. Only if I touch it."

"So you okay then?" He tugged at his beard, his worried eyes panning across me, looking for damage.

"Yeah, no problem. Hey, Johannes, I found some clothes this morning. I don't know if you want them . . ."

"*Hawu*! Where?"

"Just . . . outside. Um . . . they were . . . yeah . . . just outside this morning. Someone must have forgotten them. I thought they . . . might even have been yours."

His eyes pierced into mine. For a horrible moment I thought he was cross.

"They looked like yours . . ." My voice tailed off weakly and I looked down, fumbling with the bag. "Here."

He looked at them and then at me a few times as if he was going to explode.

During the night I hadn't thought about that. How it might offend him. But standing in front of him, it suddenly became clear how spare he must feel to have some white lightie giving him clothes.

I was just about to apologise and turn away when he burst into a loud, wet-leafy laugh and gave me a giant fire-hug, just like the day before, except this time we were laughing.

"*Hawu*! You found them eh?" He wobbled in a gale of whistling laughter. "You a funny *mnumzana*, Mike. Thank you. Ay, ay, ay, thanks very much, man. This is too good . . ."

I looked at him, relieved and grinning.

"You so cheeky, Mike, you the number one!"

I remembered Jenny. She must have been dangerously close to the bridge by then.

"I must go, I'm late. See you this arvy, maybe. Oh no, we're playing away."

"You in the team? You didn't tell me!"

"Yeah. I was too busy being a naff yesterday."

"You not the naff, you the number one *mnumzana*! And you teach those *skelems*, eh?"

"Okay."

"You tell the teacher. Don't be scared."

"Yeah," I lied. "Cheers."

"Good luck, man!" he shouted after me.

I turned round once and saw him examining the clothes, then ran to save a Crunchie's worth of pocket money.

I got a lot of nervous looks from the culprits that day. I reckon they were all just waiting for me to split on them. It was quite fun letting them stew like that, without letting on whether I was going to tell or not. Using Jenny's strategy gave me quite a kick. No wonder she did it to me so often.

The blokes were actually pretty decent to me. Trying to grease me to make sure that I wouldn't blow it for them. Trevor came over and said it was the thing that happened to everyone when they first got to the school, unless they were naffs. It was pathetically obvious that they were only greasing me to try and keep themselves out of trouble. They needn't have worried. I wouldn't sink to their slimy depths by telling on them anyway. I wasn't interested in fighting with them. But I had better things to do than waste time trying to make friends with a useless bunch of steamrolled frogs who could only fight battles when they outnumbered the enemy. I'd rather stick to having no friends at all. Or at least no friends my own age, if they were all I had to choose from.

That afternoon we had our first soccer victory of the

season. Against the useless B team of some red-and-black school above Gardens. We beat them four–nil. And I even scored the third goal. Their A team had thumped our lot in the first game of the season; but the B team was hopeless. They had a fat meatball of a goalie who shouted the odds the whole way through the game; thick things like "Leave it, goalie's ball!", so the defender would leave it, only to let Richard come steaming in and score an easy goal. He was supposed to be the captain. I ask you! Who ever heard of the goalie being captain? Mind you, just about the whole game was played in their half, so maybe it's not such a bad idea.

Anyway, it was our first victory and my first goal, and that's what counted. I didn't let Mom and Jenny know how slack the other team was, so they were really impressed when I told them about it. Anyone would think I was a World Cup player or something, the way they carried on.

I ran out to tell Johannes, but he wasn't at his shack. He was usually out at that time of the afternoon.

I did see him that evening though.

After supper Jenny and I took off in our Mosquitos on a quick, low-level bombing mission to get bread and milk for Mom. We cruised along in the clear evening sky checking our radios, and I taught Jenny a couple of the words they use, like 'roger', 'angels', 'vector' and 'over and out'. As we approached the shop, we noticed two drunk Xhosas sitting on a wall across the road, singing and shouting away.

"Don't look at them," I warned Jenny.

Drunk men make me nervous. If you look at them, they start trying to talk to you, and then if you say the wrong thing they can get cheesed off, and then you never know what might happen. So we flew on at angels 1, completely ignoring the enemy aircraft across the road. At least, that was how it went until one of them called out my name.

"Mike . . . Ay? *Mm-numzzana!*"

I couldn't believe it. One of them was Johannes, so sozzled he could hardly talk.

"Johannes!" My voice gave away my surprise, but they couldn't even tell.

I noticed he was wearing Dad's jacket and one of the shirts I gave him, but he still had his old rods on. I held my breath in case Jenny recognised them. But she didn't.

"Yyyah *mnumzana*! You . . . pretend you don't . . . n't . . . know mme? Come meet a . . . my good . . . gooood Xhosa friend." He staggered slightly and patted the other bloke on the back a hard, sloppy shot.

I had to go over and say howzit to this stinking drunk that Johannes had met somewhere. I told them I'd scored the third goal and that we won four–nil. So the bloke insisted on shaking my hand and tried to make me have a drink.

"You drink *mnumzana*? Come on, you . . . *got to* drink to the . . . goal. You jus' like . . . Teenage Dlll-Dladla!" He hiccupped, and looked at me through the top of his head as he whirled around with his foot seemingly nailed to the pavement, holding out a big, pirate-sized bottle of wine with one of those glass loop-things to hold it by.

"No thanks."

Johannes hissy-whistled into a coughing laugh and slapped me on the back. "*Ayibo* . . . Mmike's a young *mnumzana*. He's not . . . drink this *bad* stufff . . . man . . . Thiss *bad stuff*!" He gusted off into another lungful of laugh.

"Well, I reckon I must be going . . ." I said vaguely, drowned by them laughing at each other. "Cheers."

"Ay Mike . . . *mmnumzana*! Where you going?"

"I've godda get milk and things . . ."

"Go well, my friend . . . see you."

I was glad to get away. It was horrible seeing him like that.

I stood around in the shop, wishing we didn't have to go back past them. That other chap had made Johannes get drunk, I kept telling myself. He just tried to get everyone to drink that disgusting wine. I can't stand wine. Whenever I try and drink it, it sends horrible crawls up my neck, it tastes so lousy. I don't know how anyone can drink enough to make themselves drunk. One sip of it makes me want to vomit.

Luckily they'd gone by the time we went back, so we didn't have to say anything or try and ignore them, which would have made us look like idiots. But they made me completely forget that we were supposed to have been on a low level mission.

The next afternoon Johannes was on his rock at the fire. I felt a bit of a cabbage at first when I saw him, but I really didn't need to. He was back to his decent old normal self again. Apart from Dad's jacket and shirt which he was still wearing.

"Ay, ay, ay, Mike!" he said with his usual warm smile. "*Hawu*! We had a party last night, ay!" He clapped a careful hand to his forehead, shook his head and chuckled. "It was good to see you last night, Mike man. A surprise."

I sat on the spare rock next to him. "Yeah."

I almost felt guilty for not being able to say the same. And rather shamefully I realised what a skate I'd been. He was happy to see me any time, no matter what. And there I was, too bloody high and mighty (or something) to like him when he'd had a bit too much to drink. That's not what a good friend really is. Not someone who only likes you sometimes. In my own way I was actually just as snotty about certain people as Trevor and the gang. Well. I didn't really believe that, but almost.

"How was your big match, Mike? Good game? You win?" He held his hands almost together, like a frozen clap, ready to rub them together if the news was good.

"But I told . . ." I stopped myself in the nick of time as I realised he wasn't joking. He must have been so drunk that he couldn't remember a thing I'd said. "We won. I scored a goal!"

"You did?" he yelled, and his hands went off like a steam engine. "Ay, *mnumzana*, you number one! Was it a good one?"

"Eh?"

"The goal?" His eyes glowed. He was all audience, ready to hear the story again properly.

I was so glad to tell him again at the fire as if we hadn't ever been away. Everything was good again.

In the two weeks that followed I found him at the fire or in the shack most days, and we spoke about the soccer team (which I'd been made a regular member of) and how the others seemed to have been leaving me alone since the rumble at the river. He reckoned it was because I'd told the teacher, so I just said yeah.

What bugged me was the fact that he still kept wearing the same clothes. Now that he had Dad's coat and shirt, he never wore his original old ones. So one day I decided to ask him if he didn't like them any more or what.

"My old clothes?" he asked, all innocently. "No, I don't wear them any more. I like your new ones you gave me, Mike." He winked and gave me a firm pat on the shoulder that nearly knocked me off my rock.

"But why don't you wear them sometimes? I mean, for a change, sort of?"

"Well," he sighed deeply, "I think I must tell you, *mnumzana* . . . Ay, I lost them Mike. They got stolen . . . you know." He looked downwards, sort of ashamed, like as if I could tell he was lying or something.

It was the day before the July holidays, and soon he'd be going home for his two-week break. Home without any luggage. So, without thinking, I said, "I'll get you some more."

He looked up at me, all surprised, and then I knew I'd put my foot in it.

"*Hawu*! Where? You say you found this?" He tugged at the elbow of the sports coat.

"Yeah, well," I was really cornered, but we'd both got pretty good at lying to each other, "sometimes I find other clothes. Someone just leaves them around . . ."

He stared at me with a face that tried to look serious but couldn't handle the pressure, and exploded into a big laugh. "You mad, Mike. I love you!" He hugged me hard with the smell of fire, and I felt so happy it was sort of . . . sad, I suppose, you know when you feel so good about something you almost want to cry? Like that.

I got more clothes the next morning, but he wasn't there, so I just left them at the shack, hidden from the road. It was breakup day, so the schools opened floodgates at noon, pouring screaming mobs out onto the streets for three-and-a-bit weeks. Jenny rushed off with Benjy's sister, and I flew home on a solo mission. On my way past the shack, Johannes came out to meet me, wearing some of the new things and his permanent smile.

"Howzit Johannes."

"Somebody just leave them, eh Mike?" He did a head-shaking laugh. "Thanks my friend. Fits just my size."

We sat inside the shack, Johannes up on his bed and me on the creaky chair.

"I'm glad you got them. I was scared someone would swipe them."

"Ay, Mike, next holidays you must come with me to the Transkei. I want to show my family a *good mnumzana*!"

It was pretty sad to hear that, but I had to laugh. "Yeah, that would be great."

"Spot on! And fishing, man, fishing in the sea . . ." His mouth smacked open and his eyes rolled. "There's lots of good people in the Transkei . . . my friends . . . and you learn to speak good Xhosa . . ."

I nodded. I'd never be allowed to go, but it sounded pretty good. Then the blokes would probably get at me because I fished with Xhosas. Fishing with Xhosas in the Transkei and best friends with a Zulu in Greytown. They'd probably die of shock. Better than fishing with them, any day.

". . . And lots to eat and drink . . . no police. No . . ." His eyes slowly closed as he drifted off into a long, fond silence.

"No christenings," I said, tugging him back cruelly, back from the paradise he hardly ever got to see.

"Eh?"

"In the river. No christenings."

"Ohh. Yah, Mike. No *bed* stuff, man. *Hawu*, long time

ago . . . it was not so bad . . . no so bad as today. Today, it's *very bed*, not like when I was a young . . ." He drifted back to the distant past, glazed eyes staring beyond the dusty window panes.

I sat softly twanging at the wire under the seat of the chair. Then I spotted a cloth bag beneath the table stuffed with the clothes he'd worn for the past two weeks, so I picked it up, making a spur of the moment decision. He looked at me apprehensively.

"I'll wash 'em."

"Ay, no, Mike. It's okay. I go to the laundry now, after I see you, anyway."

"But I can do it for nothing. We've got a washing-machine at home. It's best that I do them." I searched for some sort of excuse, "Just this once, while you think about our holiday. Okay?"

He didn't seem too pleased to let me do it, but he didn't argue. I don't reckon he had money to waste on washing, I could tell that much. I mean, you'd have to be pretty thick to think that Johannes had money to spend on laundry.

I reckon deep down he was actually quite pleased to have his stuff done for him. The only problem was that I had to do it without getting caught.

Jenny was at a friend's that afternoon, so although it was almost drizzly outside, I decided to get on with it while the trouble was away. When the blackmailer's away, the big brothers play. (I know that's not the right version, but that's what it should really say.)

The hardest part about operating the washing-machine was trying to work out how to open the stupid door thing. I pulled at it till the handle almost broke before realising that you have to lift a secret, zizzy-nopple type of catch first. I reckon they put it there to trick people.

I stuffed the clothes and the bag in, all in a lump as they were. The washing-machine churned around so much, they would come apart anyway. The only thing that worried me was how long the sports coat would take to dry. I'd have to hide it in the shed while it did so. It would get a bit covered in spider webs and stuff, but that was the only place no one went to.

I'd seen Mom doing the washing, so I pulled the little drawer open and chucked some powder into two of the pigsties. I even knew which sty to put that blue stuff into, because it had stains from all the times before.

"Johannes, your clothes are gonna be really *soft*!" I said to myself, pouring plenty of the stuff in.

I had to put the bottle down to rub my hands together with glee. It's mad to say it, but I was really enjoying myself. I shnick-shnick-shnicked the program nopple round to about where Mom puts it, and then switched on. The red light came on and I stood back to watch the thing in action.

Nothing happened. Maybe it had to warm up before it did anything, I thought, but it had taken too long even for that. I looked at the sink, then laughed out aloud and actually felt a bit of a cabbage for being so thick, even though no one could see me. I'd forgotten to connect the hoses to the taps. It was all quite simple, really. The red one was for the hot tap and the blue one for the cold. You'd have to be a total idiot to get anything wrong. Apart from the stupid catch on the door thing, I suppose.

As soon as I switched the taps on we were in business, as Dad used to say. There was hissing and a click, and the thing started churning even before the water had finished drowning the bag.

I watched for a while to see the clothes getting set free, but it took too long and soon got boring, so I went out and checked the shed to see if it would be okay to hang things in. It was a bity musty but not too bad. I could steal a few hangers to put the clothes on and hang them from garden forks and planks and things if I stuck them in the right places.

Then I declared war on the spiders with a spade, only stopping when a window nearly got broken, but by then the place was pretty clear of webs, and I reckon the spiders had got the message loud and clear that they weren't wanted there.

When I passed the kitchen, the machine was humming and sloshing away like an electric stomach. I checked to see how we were doing for time, then settled down to read while it finished.

After a few pages I heard the first rinse draining out and the taps hissing away again. As long as Jenny didn't come home too early, it would be dead easy. I decided that if she caught me I'd say I was doing our own washing to help Mom a bit, like they say you're supposed to at cubs or scouts or something. Then I'd just have to put an extra load of our own stuff in and sneak Johannes's out to the shed.

Two rinses later I could still hear it churning away, so I started to get worried. The thing was taking too long for comfort, so I got up to check how many more numbers the thing had to go before crossing the finishing line.

As I reached the kitchen it started its fourth flood.

Yeah, I said flood, not rinse. I nearly flipped. The whole floor was a lake. Even the passage carpet was totally soaked. It squelched underfoot as I ran to the rescue. The drain hose was gushing water straight onto the floor, spraying up onto the wall and fridge as it jetted out from its position, still hooked behind the machine.

How the hell are you supposed to remember to put *three* hoses in the sink? Anyway, it was too late to complain about stupid washing-machine designs, the damage was done. I hooked the drain hose over the sink (for what it was worth at that stage), then started mopping up with newspapers and cloths while I interviewed the men inside my head about how to get out of the fine mess I was in.

They came up with something that wasn't such a bad idea after all. Johannes's wash was nearly finished — judging by the floor, that was fairly obvious. So when it finished, I put a load of our own clothes in and put them on to wash quickly before anyone got home. Then I would own up to the mess

(I could hardly blame anyone else), but I wouldn't get into too much trouble because I was only trying to be helpful.

It worked. Apart from having another fight with that pathetic catch thing because it wouldn't open for about ten minutes after the wash, the plan went off perfectly. They didn't even suspect I'd been doing someone else's washing. I suppose no one in their right mind would do someone else's washing anyway.

All I had to do was dry the carpet as much as possible with a cloth. And now I don't think anyone will ever ask me to do the washing again, so I reckon it was worth it!

Chapter 9

A birthday surprise

One thing I didn't want anyone to know about was my birthday.

Every time it was somebody's birthday, Mr Laing would announce it to the whole class, and that person would have to feel a real prune while they sang "Happy Birthday" and laughed and teased. Then the Birthday Person would get sort of special treatment for the rest of the day.

That was something I didn't need. It was bad enough as it was, with them always thinking that I got special treatment from Mr Laing.

I reckoned they wouldn't know about mine because I was new to the school, and they'd been there for years. So on the morning of August the first, as we crossed the bridge to school, I wasn't too worried. And just to be safe, I made Jenny promise not to tell anyone. I really should have known better though, as I soon found out.

I'd nearly forgotten about it myself by the time Mr Laing and his dusty file came into the classroom. But *he* hadn't.

"Morning class, sit down," he said, breezing into the room. "Open some windows please, Andy. And whose birthday is it today?"

Everyone started looking at each other to see whose it was. I tried to act normal and hoped that my ears had made a mistake. Or that it was also someone else's birthday. But his terrible eyes aimed straight at me. Gradually every head swivelled in my direction until I reckon even the spiders and things were looking.

"Mr Goodenough!"

His voice sounded miles away. My face went red-hot, and still I didn't look up.

"Let's sing him a Happy Birthday, shall we?"

He started off in an embarrassingly loud, cheerful voice, and the rest of the class tagged along reluctantly. Then there were three half-hearted cheers that sounded more like boos to me as I studied the wood grain and fish drawings on my desk. I could feel eyes burning hate into me as if it was my fault for having a birthday, so I didn't look up for a long time. Not until the lesson was well under way.

Of course the blokes had to make clever comments about it during break time. Andy asked me if I thought I was a main ou just because I was the same age as him, and someone shouted something about me not being a piglet any more, which everyone thought was really funny. That's how pathetic they were. They reckoned I was big enough to eat out of rubbish bins now, instead of troughs, which was supposed to be another hilarious joke.

Trevor said, "Now you're almost old enough to go camping," as if that was a big deal, just because they were planning to camp in Newlands Forest over the weekend.

"Yeah," said Mally from behind Trevor's shoulder. "If you weren't such an overgrown naff, you could have come with us."

"You're too much of a chicken," Andy chipped in. "If you came with us, your chattering teeth would keep us awake all night."

Then there were more roars of scathing laughter, as if they thought they were the greatest hero comedians of all time.

"I wouldn't want to camp with you lot, anyway," I muttered and walked away.

Actually, to tell the truth, it sounded quite exciting to me. It was the sort of thing that made me wish Phocho lived round the corner so that we could do all those things too. And do them much better than Trevor and his feeble gang of main ou slimeballs ever could.

"And we can't have pigs eating our whole midnight feast!" Mally shouted as I disappeared round the corner.

The mad thing about them was the way they would change their minds about me whenever they felt like it. Usually they were pretty decent to me the day after they'd been lousy, almost as if it was some kind of carefully worked out pattern, to sort of balance things out or something. But later I decided that it was only my imagination. There was no pattern to the way they handled me. They just did what they liked when they liked. And it was the day after my birthday that made me decide that.

When I got to school, almost all the blokes came charging up to me in a big, excited gang with the four campers, Trevor, Mally, Andy and Leon, up front.

"Hey Pig!" Andy shouted. "We've come to make friends!"

My first thought was that it must be a trick, then I wondered if they were going to ask me to camp with them, because they knew I was an outdoor type. I mean, they all knew that I could shoot, ride and catch fish, so maybe they thought I'd come in handy at the camp if anything went wrong.

They crowded round and Trevor held out a decently wrapped present with a shiny paper ribbon on it. "We didn't know it was going to be your birthday yesterday, so that's why it's late, but this is for you from all of us."

I didn't know what to say.

It was a small present, about the size of a lunch-box. At first I thought it might have just been empty because it was light, but when I shook it something bumped around inside. Everyone looked distressed as I rattled it, so I stopped in case something broke.

There was a piece of card on it which had been written very neatly, probably by one of the girls. It said: "To Pig, Happy Birthay from all of us in Std 5." It had been written so slowly and carefully that whoever wrote it had left the 'd' out of 'Birthday'.

Everyone watched me with bright, expectant faces, and for once I felt really special. Nobody said a word. Someone in the background bounced a tennis ball, but apart from that they waited quietly for me to say something or open the present.

"Thanks," I stammered, trying to think of what to say. "I really didn't expect you to . . . to give me anything. I mean . . . I'm really . . . it's nice . . . you shouldn't have. I think we've been rumbling for too long. I've always wanted to make friends." For a horrible moment I thought I was actually going to cry. "You've christened me and we've had our bad times, but we're actually all the same kind of ous really. Like . . . Phocho is a really good bloke too . . . I reckon you'd agree . . . if you met him, you'd realise . . ." A few of them shifted as I spoke, as if they felt guilty about having been so lousy in the past. "Maybe one day you can all come up to Greytown on a sort of . . . camping and fishing trip. You can meet Phocho . . . and even go shooting . . ." I looked at Mally. "Even you, Mally . . . I reckon you could learn how to shoot quite well." My voice quivered slightly. He looked down and kicked at the ground.

"Open it!" someone called out.

"Yeah!" Everyone looked keenly at the present again.

"Okay," I said.

I was sort of hoping not to have to open it in front of them in case it was something I didn't really like, and then I'd have to pretend to be pleased with it. I hate doing that. That's why I prefer Christmas, because then everyone else is too busy opening their own presents to notice you.

I said thanks again, then carefully unstuck the tape and took the paper off. It was an orange and white lunch box, a second-hand one, but I realised it was only the packaging for what was inside.

Everyone had taken a nervous step back from me, and suddenly I sensed that something was horribly wrong. A tense silence had come over them. There wasn't a movement or a breath as they waited for the big moment. I paused, but it was too late to change my mind, I'd gone too far. So I took a nervous breath and pulled the lid off.

They gasped at what they saw, and immediately a choking, lethal pong hit the air. Inside, against the horrible orange plastic, lay a grisly mess, like something from a horror movie. I blinked in disbelief at the twisted remains of a flattened rat. They must have picked it up off the road. The eyes and skin from the face were gone, and the guts had turned black from rotting in the sun. Tiny things darted about over the stinking fur and broken teeth.

"Kaffir food!" someone yelled.

All around there were whoops and howls of delight. I stared, and they laughed like hell. Others asked to see, then joined in the vicious chorus. Someone flicked the bottom of the box, causing horrified screams as the rat bounced out against my shirt and fell to the ground. Then they charged off like a roaring stampede of sick animals to play stingers.

Suddenly I was totally alone. Burny vomit lurched up and stopped in the back of my throat. I stared at the rat and my eyes went blurry wet. Swearwords swarmed in my head.

I hated myself. I should have known it would be a trick. My fists clenched till my nails cut, trying to fight the crying.

The Standard Fours watched me from the netball field. They must have been really thick if they thought I couldn't tell. I turned my back on them so they couldn't see, then knelt down to scrape the rat back into the box. I walked up past the prefabs, stopping to dump the box and wrapping paper in a bin with all the other greaseproof paper and apple cores, as if it was nothing.

Peter Green was leaning against the wall ahead of me, in the same place as I saw him on my first day. He seemed to be the only one who hadn't had anything to do with the trick as far as I could tell. He was also the only one not playing stingers.

I had to talk to someone, so I went over to him even though he was a bit of a naff. At least he was decent enough to keep out of the stinking tricks the others played on me.

"Have they been pushing you around again?" he asked, showing quite an unusual willingness to talk.

"Yeah, thought it was a huge joke, putting a stupid rat in an old lunch-box."

"They did that to me once," he said casually. "I was going

to warn you, but they got to you first. It's their favourite trick."

"Oh."

It came as a bit of a surprise to me. Suddenly I felt much better. It helped a lot to know that I wasn't the only one, and for the first time I realised I wasn't. There was someone who'd been noticing everything all along. Even if he was a naff, I decided, he's a pretty decent bloke.

"Somebody should attack their *big camp* over the week-end," he muttered spitefully. He said "big camp" all sarcastic as if he thought it was pathetically childish. "Tear them to shreds. I hope they get murdered or something! I reckon they deserve it."

I looked at him, all amazed at how wound up he was getting. I didn't know he had it in him to get so cheesed off about something. But his words sounded good to me because I felt exactly the same way.

"Yeah, let's!" I said, getting all worked up at the idea.

"My dad says we should leave them alone though . . . reckons it's just asking for trouble having anything to do with them."

I noticed that Peter included me by using the word "we".

So some people did know what went on. Ever since Dad died I'd had a silly feeling that Johannes was the only one who ever realised what happened to me any more. You can't let moms know about what goes on at school. They'd have heart attacks if you did. It's only dads and close friends that you can tell, really.

"Well, we won't mention it to him then, eh?" I said, too keen to let the plan just drop. "Tell you what: I've got a good friend who would definitely help us!" I was really buzzing. "He's really brilliant. And big too. I bet he'll help us get our own back on them. He knows how raw they've been to me and always reckons we should teach them a lesson or two. So now when I say we want to, he'll help us! What do you say?"

"Well . . ." Peter seemed a bit scared once it started to look like more than just words. "Who's this ou?"

110

"Bloke called Johannes. I see him at the soccer fields sometimes. He's a really good ou . . .'

"You mean the boy who does the grounds?" Peter said, staring in disbelief.

"He's not a boy, he's a man." I noticed Peter looking a bit put off. "He's just like anyone else. He's a really nice bloke, I'm telling you . . . Why don't you come and meet him this afternoon, an' you'll see what I mean."

"I can't."

Peter was trying to get out of it, I could just tell, but I wasn't going to let him get away with it.

"Why not?"

"I've got to go to a piano lesson."

I stared at him in shock and horror. "I didn't know you played the piano?" It was a really naff kind of thing to do, playing the piano.

"Yeah, every Thursday, but don't tell anyone. I don't let them know."

"What time's your lesson?"

"Four o'clock."

"Well then you've got stacks of time. Just come down to the field to check him after school. Just for ten minutes. Then you can decide whether you wanna be in on the plan or not, 'cause I'm definitely gonna do it!"

That really got him keen on the whole thing. He didn't want to miss out on anything, and if I was going to do it, he'd have to do it too. To tell the truth, I would never have had the guts to do it on my own, but he wasn't to know.

"Okay," he said cautiously, "but I won't be able to stay for long, eh?"

"Nah. It won't take long," I said, beginning to feel as big as a house. Things were really starting to happen at last. I could feel the good old electricity racing in my bones again for the first time in ages.

Chapter 10

Night raid

We hurried down to the fields straight after the last bell, but Johannes was nowhere to be seen. I felt a bit of a prune for having talked Peter into coming, because it looked as if I'd been sprouting about the whole thing.

"So where's he?" Peter challenged.

"I dunno. He's normally somewhere around . . ."

I swivelled my head, scanning the edges of the ground, desperately hoping to spot him before Peter lost interest.

"Well, I'm gonna have to go then. I can't wait too long, else I'll miss the late bus as well."

He turned to leave.

"Wait!" I grabbed him by the sleeve. "He's got to be somewhere close by. Let's just go and look round near the café first."

But I could tell Peter was getting chicken.

"I reckon I've godda go, mun, I'll get into . . ."

He was interrupted by a distant voice behind us.

"*Molo!*" it said, unmistakably Johannes. "Where you going?"

I felt so relieved. I'd really wanted Peter so see that Johannes was a decent bloke, and not some sort of animal like they all thought he was.

He strode up to us in his usual cheerful manner.

"Johannes," I said, all official like at a dinner party for fossils or something, "this is a friend of mine, Peter."

"Hello Johannes," Peter said nervously, as if he thought maybe he ate people.

"Ay, very pleased. How are you, *mnumzana*?"

He shot a big friendly hand out for Peter to shake.

"All right thanks," said Peter, shaking it as if it were made of glass.

I wanted to laugh, but I knew it would make Peter feel a bit of a chop, so I didn't.

Johannes traversed to me, eyes glowing. "So you do it at last then, Mike?" he said, nodding at Peter. "You make good with the other *mnumzanas*, Mike?"

"No, not really," I said.

Peter looked totally confused.

"Only with Peter. The others thought they were huge jokers today, gave me a present with a dead rat in it."

Johannes laughed a bit, then checked himself. "Sorry. It's just funny, Mike. I know it's not funny . . . but it's just *funny*!"

Suddenly it did seem funny. I mean, they didn't hit me or anything. They just played a stupid trick. I started to laugh, and so did Peter, then Johannes joined in again, with his big, wheezing guffaw. We watched each other laughing and just kept on, each of us making the other giggle all the more. Johannes's beard rippled. He shook his head and slapped his thigh like a cowboy as he laughed. And I laughed at him laughing, like Phocho and I did in the old days.

"We've got an idea for a trick on them," Peter piped up at last, suddenly much more confident.

"Ohh yah?" He looked at us with keen question marks in his eyes. "What you do?"

"The main ous are going on a camp in Newlands Forest this weekend," I began.

"Yah, yah?" Johannes was really interested.

"And we wanna raid their camp!" Peter burst out.

"How?"

We stared at each other for a moment.

"Uh," I looked from Peter to Johannes. "We hadn't worked that part out yet . . . we thought maybe you'd be able to help us . . . you know . . . ideas . . . what to do?"

He sat forward, clasped his hands together with a deep clap and looked at us seriously.

"How many camping?"

"Four."

"Four? *Hawu, mnumzana*, that's easy! Easy, easy. We make one bad *tokoloshe* for them. Just one . . ." At this stage he sniffed a huge gale of air, his eyes caught fire, and he let out a blood-ripping Dracula laugh, complete with wet leaf whistly sounds. It was so loud it echoed on the clubhouse and got a few dogs barking. ". . . And they wish they were never born!"

As I turned to Peter, he smiled at me. We just knew it would work.

"That's excellent!" I whooped. "Will you do it for us?"

"Will I do it? I do it for you *any time*! I do it to the *skelems*." He hung a hand on Peter's shoulder. "Any time for a friend, and *mnumzanas* like you are always my friends." He stretched his other arm out and gave me a double-jerk type of squeeze.

"Yeeha!" we screamed, "let's get them!"

We laughed again. Then Johannes rubbed his hands together and said we had to make plans.

Peter missed the late bus in the end because we got so carried away with all the organising, and he had to make up some excuse about being kept in by Mr Laing.

He had some careful talking to do to get his fossils to let him kip at our place on Saturday night. Then we were to meet Johannes in the park at ten and walk to the forest.

The next morning was pathetic. Trevor, Mally, Andy and Leon really thought they were the main ous. It was Friday, their last chance to brag about the Big Camp, and they only shouted off about it. The crazy thing was that everyone else listened as if it was front page news.

A few blokes looked at me all guilty as if they realised that the rat trick was a bit of a raw one to pull on anybody, but I just pretended nothing had happened. To tell the truth, I'd almost forgotten the whole thing because I was so excited about raiding their camp.

From the quad entrance I spotted Peter arriving at the front gate. If he couldn't kip over, the whole raid would be off, so I stood there holding my breath and hoping. He didn't look all that happy. But then again he never really looked happy, so maybe it didn't mean anything. From about twenty paces away he noticed me, looked toward the netball fields where the gang buzzed around the campers like teenybopper fans, then looked back at me, slightly raising one eyebrow.

"And?" I asked.

He stole another glance to make sure no one was watching, then showed me a thumbs up fist which he clapped into his open hand. "It's on!" he said with a secret smile, "the mission's underway!"

"Excellent!" I hissed, and we stalked off to discuss our plans.

Peter's fossils had arranged to drop him off at our place on the Saturday afternoon, so we had time to watch some of the club's soccer teams playing league matches. We found Johannes watching the games from the far side of the field as usual, and went over to meet him.

"*Molo!*" He seemed just about as excited as us about the whole plan.

"So we'll see you here tonight at ten, eh?" I checked.

"Yah. Yah, Mike, at ten."

We went off after soccer and had an early supper, then pretended to be tired, to make sure Jenny wouldn't try and stay up with us. We watched TV with Mom for a while, but I couldn't concentrate on a thing. Time dragged by pathetically slowly. I noticed that Peter was also thinking about later on. Every now and then he'd peep in my direction to see if I was watching the TV properly or not. And Jenny kept hanging around, staring at us as if we were about to suddenly put on a circus act for her or something. I suppose it had been ages since a friend came round for the night. Not since Phocho.

Eventually Mom sent her off to bed, which caused a huge commotion of whining and stuff, but at least it got her out of the way. By about quarter to ten we were really feeling wound up, but we reckoned to Mom we were going to kip.

"All right, darling" she said.

I could have just about crawled under the couch. How could she go and say "darling" in front of Peter? He didn't seem to notice, though. Or at least he didn't say anything, which was a bit of luck.

We shut the door and put the light out, then quietly started pulling on our black clothes which we'd especially picked for night camouflage.

"We've godda be extra quiet when we go out the window," I whispered, "'cause Jenny's room's right next door, and she's got ears like Drac when it comes to doing something wrong."

Peter giggled.

"Ssh!"

I was already beginning to feel a bit shaky, but I didn't let on.

The window pushed open smoothly and quietly because I'd oiled it especially that morning. Peter went through the burglar guards first, making a bit too much noise for comfort. I held onto the back end of him as he sort of hung out the window, twisting and squirming his way through. Suddenly he slid out of my hands just like a fish, and hit the shrubs head first with a rustling twig-crackle and a groan. I still had one of his shoes in my hand. The noise frightened me, froze me while I checked if Jenny had heard. But the only sounds came from below where Peter was trying to separate himself from the mud and plants. He was hissing like a steam engine. At first I thought it was crying, but then I realised he was having a muted fit of giggles. I looked at the shoe and then I started too. We stared at one another in the darkness, choking snorts of laughter.

Luckily I got through okay, otherwise Jenny would definitely have woken up. We flew in formation along the pavement towards the soccer club, only I didn't tell Peter that we were actually two Lancasters. I kept it to myself in case he thought it was stupid.

A horrible feeling told me that Johannes might not be there, but I needn't have worried. He'd spotted us coming and was out on the pavement ready and waiting for us.

"You been too long, *mnumzana*!" he said under his breath.

"Well, here we are, ready for action!"

It was funny, we were all whispering even though there was no one about who could have heard us.

He clapped his hands into a vice. "We go now."

As we started walking, he dug into his coat pocket and pulled out a little shopping packet with something heavy inside.

"Here, this one for you," he said, shoving it into Peter's hands. "I have lots for us."

"What's it?" I asked.

"It's stones. Small stones from the road, *mnumzana*. First we give the *skelems* a nice shower!"

He didn't look at us, just stared straight ahead and started walking faster.

"Yareeeevaa!" we screamed. "Let's *go*!".

We skipped and danced around Johannes, yelling war cries and really getting into the mood.

It was almost an hour's walk, and we'd quietened down by the time we got to the edge of the forest, so we sat for a rest and made final plans. Peter knew more or less where they would be because he'd run school cross-countries in the forest and heard that they'd be near the starting point, so he was made official scout with the job of finding the camp. Then we'd get into position, throw two handfuls of gravel each, Johannes would do his horror laugh, and then we'd hit cover and lie low till they went back to bed. Maybe we'd have to fight with them, but at least Johannes was on our side. He might have been old, but he was as tough as a rhino.

"Okay, so let's go then," I said, trying to disguise the shakiness.

We tiptoed up the twisted track. In motionless silence the trees hung over us, wondering what we wanted. The close darkness gave me the creeps, but I pretended it didn't. It was okay walking along the road with streetlights and all, but suddenly I felt as if I really was a naff, and that they must be pretty brave to just camp in the forest. I mean, anything could happen. Like murderers could be lurking about, or some lost leopard or something.

"Stop!" I hissed.

We froze.

"What?" Johannes asked.

I thought I'd heard a rustling sound in the bushes just off the road, but it was probably my imagination, so I said, "It's gone now," and carried on walking, my heart pounding as if it wanted to escape or something.

"The spot's not far ahead," Peter whispered.

We stopped to listen for a while. Nothing. Then as we began to move again, there was a sound.

"Wait!"

Distant muffled laughter drifted up between the craggy trunks. We looked towards it, and at once spotted the pale glow. It was their tent all right. A gas lamp inside turned the shape into a giant Chinese lantern. From where we were it was just visible through the tangle of twigs and branches. The pine trees huddled into a soundless black ceiling above us as we closed in on our target. My knees were like rubber butterflies, but I realised that Peter probably felt the same, so it didn't worry me too much.

The voices were pretty clear as we got closer, but not quite enough to hear what they were saying. Every minute or so Andy's laugh exploded above the churning words of Trevor and Mally, then he'd shout in a few comments and leave a dotted line for them to carry on talking.

Leon seemed to be keeping fairly quiet. For a horrible moment I imagined he was on guard duty outside somewhere, but then his slippery voice chipped in too.

We inched forward through the rotty leaves and stuff they

taught us about in Standard Three, stopping dead for a while each time someone cracked a twig, to make sure they hadn't heard us.

The tent was almost within range.

We hardly breathed, easing past ticklish sprays of shrub, making little clearings with our toes before putting our feet down to stop the crackles.

Johannes leant over to me and whispered, using only his breathing to talk with: "There," he pointed, "is the best place."

He'd chosen a spot with good cover exactly behind the tent, so that if they came out they'd have their backs to us. We edged round towards the place while the voices murmured and muffled away inside the glowing target. We stopped at the low bushes behind the tent and dug into the gravel packets, trying to make as little sound as possible.

I stared at Peter. He stared at me. Johannes smiled at us, then whispered, "Okay *mnumzana*, let's give it to them!"

I stood up and launched my first fistful. The small stones made a *scritch* noise as they left my hand, and then there was nothing, just the sound of the voices inside the enemy target. It seemed to take forever for them to land, but finally they started raining down, first dinking off the twigs above, and then in loud thuds onto the canvas and peppering the forest all round.

The voices cut dead instantly.

My heart went into overdrive. I wanted to run before it was too late. Then Johannes threw off both fistfuls, *scritch*, *scritch*, so did Peter, and then I launched off my other load. In seconds the forest was raining pebbles. Salvo after salvo. All over the tent they drummed and through the trees they clicked, richocheting and rustling into the dead leaves.

Inside the tent a quavery voice broke the silence with a nervous, "Hhhey!"

Then Johannes did his laugh: "**Boooo**-hoo-hoo-hoo-hoo-huh-huh-huh-huh-haaaAAAAAA!"

It nearly made *me* die of fright, never mind them!

Someone inside the tent tried to say "Hey" again, but it just didn't come out right. It was more like a sort of a frightened, pants-wetting scream. Then a desperate voice hissed "Let's go!", and the tent erupted into a puffing, prodding bag of urgent elbows and things as they fought for the door. There was a clatter and a thud, a few groans, then suddenly four pale, tracksuited figures burst from the tent and launched off down the hill, making horrible shouting noises as they ran.

I knew what they were going through. They must have felt just like Phocho and I did the day we thought we saw a ghost on Porcupine Hill. Maybe even worse.

We looked at each other, then burst into fitful snorts of giggles. We'd all been so scared that the giggles just broke the banks and flooded on and on. It was a wonderful feeling, as if in a dream. I never thought the day would come when I could make Trevor, Mally, Andy and Leon charge off down the hill screaming for their lives.

"Let's go'n have a look at the enemy barracks!" I suggested.

"Yah," Johannes laughed, "yah, let's see what makes a *skelem* !"

We tramped round to the front of the deserted tent. The lamp was still burning, and its bleaching light revealed a hilarious sight. We'd caught them right in the middle of their midnight feast, and things had been scattered everywhere during the escape. Smarties lay dotted all over the ground sheet, a half-eaten Crunchie had been thrown aside, a tub had taken a tumble, leaving popcorn strewn over someone's pillow, and a sarmie lay squashed into the ground just outside the doorway. But the best thing of all was the cake.

Someone's mom had made a really larney cake for them with creamy icing, cherries, decorated edges, the lot. It sat like a prize in the middle of the tent on a big Tupperware lid, just waiting to be sliced. But someone had put a foot right into it in the rush to get outside. It was a bare foot too. You could see the outline of the toes and all where they'd tromped into the icing and made a skid-mark across the lid onto the sleeping bag.

I reckon it was the funniest thing I'd ever seen. We really hooted at that, pointing at the cake and just cracking up till tears came to our eyes. And we didn't stop talking about it all the way home.

Johannes turned off at his shack and we carried on home, sneaking into the garden through the hedge. We climbed back in through the window, cleaned up a bit, and told each other the story again and again until we talked ourselves to sleep.

Mission more than just "accomplished" I'd say!

Chapter 11

Put your foot in it

We agreed not to say a word about the raid to anyone at school. It was pretty obvious that the main ous would just try and get us back in some way if they found out. We were dying to hear what they'd have to say about it all, but I must say I wasn't prepared for what came out that Monday morning. Their version was even more of a hoot than we expected.

When I got to the classroom to drop off my books and stuff, I found Trevor positioned crosslegged on Mr Laing's table, sounding off at full volume to a whole audience. Even the girls were listening to his ridiculous sprout-story. It was still quite early, and Leon hadn't turned up yet, but Andy and Mally stood next to him, nodding vigorously as the lies got more amazing by the minute.

". . . There were five or six of them," he was saying.

"No, more than that, at least seven that I could count," Mally interrupted.

"Yeah, about seven huge kaffirs. Escaped convicts with knives and things," (big serious nods all round) "and I reckon they wanted food and weapons from us."

"An' they probably also wanted to murder us!" Mally chirped, "'cause they were escaped murderers from Pollsmoor."

"Yeah," said Trevor, slightly irritated by the interruptions. "Anyway, they attacked the tent with stones and knives. It was raw, you check, they were trying to kill us with rocks and things, so we had to fight them off. I shouted at them and told them to get the hell out or we'd kill them . . ."

"An' I told them to bugger off," Andy cut in, looking at Trevor for approval.

"Yeah, an' then we ran at them with our sticks, and Leon had a huge hunting knife . . . shouting like crazy to scare them even more."

Everyone's eyes were just about on stalks.

"An' they just turned and ran, shouting 'Please don't kill us, please don't hurt us!'"

There were cheers and laughs all round.

I looked up from where I'd been shoving books away, pretending not to be interested. I couldn't believe it! And the most pathetic thing was that everyone else could. They roared and chuckled and clapped as he told the amazing tale. Pity Peter hadn't arrived in time to enjoy the wild adventures of Trevor and the main ous. It was too much!

Their story was so far-fetched, it just couldn't be left unchallenged. Of course it would only mean trouble, but I couldn't help it, it was too wonderful a moment to miss. So before I knew what was happening, I'd moved nearer, and started to act all interested, clearing my throat to attract their attention.

"When was this, Trevor?"

"None o' your business, Pig," he sneered.

"Yeah," Mally added, "you're too much of a ninny to hear about stuff like this. You'd have nightmares for the rest of your life if we told you."

Everyone laughed. They always hosed themselves at the feeble things he said, as if he was the prize comedian, especially when he said things about me.

I gave him a vicious go-and-die look and said "I didn't ask for your opinion" with so much strength that he shut up in shock and turned to Trevor to see what he was going to do about it. I also turned to Trevor, determined to carry on: "Was this at your camp in the forest?"

"Yeah," he said grudgingly.

"Somebody come and attack your camp?"

"They tried to, but we got rid of them quick enough."

"Yeah," Andy chirped up, "scared the hell out of them. They thought it was gonna be lights out *one* time!"

"Just like it will be for you one day, if you're not careful," Mally growled at me from behind Trevor.

"Oh yeah?" I scoffed at him, then carried on interviewing Trevor: "With knives an' things, eh?"

"Yeah. All we had was sticks. An' Leon had a knife, but we didn't even use it."

"Didn't you blokes nip yourselves just a little bit?"

"Nah, we're not naffs, Pig," Mally dug again.

Trevor glanced at him and nodded. "Yeah, we were okay. Reckon you might've died of fright, though."

"So no one stepped in the cake and spilt the Smarties then?" I asked.

Andy's jaw dropped. Mally's face went visibly pale, and Trevor stared at me in stunned silence.

I looked back at them, almost feeling sorry for them, almost wanting to laugh, but keeping a perfectly straight face. They made a fine sight. It was a glorious moment that hung horribly slowly, sort of frozen for them. For me it was better than any chocolate éclair or jam doughnut, better by miles than their big, creamy-iced cherry cake. Even better than seeing them charging down the hill like cowards, the way they always said I was.

And the funniest thing was that none of the onlookers knew how much was happening between us.

"Who told . . . Who said that?" Trevor stuttered, recovering just enough to speak.

"No one," I said with a casual smile, "I just made it up!" Then I walked off, leaving a flabbergasted trio of not-so-main ous and a confused audience in my wake.

I looked back once and noticed Trevor still staring at me. It might just have been my imagination, but he had a strange expression on his face, like as if he thought maybe I wasn't actually such a wet after all.

Chapter 12

The final battle

On Tuesday all the talk changed from murderers with knives to the big match of the afternoon, because we were playing the Uplands A team again.

Our blokes had got thrashed five–nil at Uplands in the first game of the season.But that was before my time, so I didn't know what they were like. Francis reckoned that we were in for an even worse thumping than last time, because they'd missed stacks of chances then and it could easily have been about eight–nil.

Mally was all cheesed off because I'd been picked to play right wing again, and he was only reserve. He said, "Yah, Pig, you're just gonna give the bloody game away. You're such a suction, that's the only reason Drac puts you in the team," which was about the usual sort of thing for him to say, I suppose.

"How do I suck up to him?" I demanded, because I knew he had no answer to that. So he just started to imitate me in this really childish voice that sounded nothing like me.

"Please sir, can I do that for you? Ooh, Mr Laing, you're such a nice teacher, I do all my homework for you, suction, suction, grease, grease. And you always call him Mr Laing, you're too chicken to call him Drac."

"So, I've never noticed you calling him Drac to his face?"
"So what?"

The argument got totally silly, so I just walked away. Of course he had to shout, "chicken!" at my back, once I was a safe distance away.

Trevor was a lot more decent about the match. He actually came up to me and planned a bit for the game.

"Hey Pig," he said, "you haven't seen these ous play yet, eh?"

"No, not their A team. They're supposed to be pretty hot, I hear?"

"Nah," he snorted, "we can chop them easily if we play right. An' that's what I want to tell you about. They're good in the centre, especially at the back, so we must keep the play right out on the wings until the last minute, when we get into their goal area, then you must come in." His fingers twisted and flicked as he spoke, becoming whichever players he needed them to be, and then he karate-chopped his left hand for emphasis: "Send in quick, neat crosses along the ground, an' I'll put them away, you'll see!" He clicked his fingers twice as he said 'put them away', and he actually smiled. I reckon it was the first time he'd ever smiled at me. Apart from laughing at me, that is.

Maybe it was my imagination, but I didn't think so somehow. There seemed to be a glimmer of something in him that had never been there before. I mean, just the fact that he was talking to me was a miracle. And then something else that I didn't expect happened. He bent closer to me, and spoke in a hushed voice.

"'Cause Mally doesn't know how to play down the wing, you know, he always tries to dribble the ball into the centre and go for the goal like a big glory boy."

I stared at him, trying to tell if he was having me on or not, like maybe he was just waiting for me to agree so that he could run off to Mally and cause more trouble. But somehow it didn't seem like a trick this time. Still, I was too wise to risk leaving myself wide open again, so I didn't agree or disagree. I just said, "Okay, I'll keep down the wing all the way."

"Oh yeah, and another thing," he added. "Their left back is quite useless, so that'll make it even better to play down your side, and we can let Benjy come in from the left wing to help me, Andy and Richard in the middle. That's if it's the same naff playing left back. You must just go straight at him. He's a big fat chicken. He should really be in the B team, but his old man's probably the coach or something."

It was amazing. Trevor was as much of a skate as the worst of them, but he'd actually really made me feel like getting out there and playing the best game of my life.

Quite funny really, because the day before, when I'd seen Johannes on the bridge on my way home from school, he'd put me right off. When he heard it was Uplands A, he reckoned we must just try and stop them from scoring too many goals. Said we didn't really have much chance of winning. He wasn't trying to be nasty or anything. He just reckoned that they always had one of the best teams in the league and we should just try for a draw.

"Good luck, Mike *mnumzana*," he said. "I won't be there to see you. Go well, my friend."

He was on his way to Crossroads to spend two nights and a day with his nephew for the big stay-away. There was going to be some protest or other, and all the black workers had to stay away from work for the day. He reckoned there'd be lots of trouble and police charges and stuff, and if anyone dared to go to work, they'd get into huge trouble from the other black blokes holding the strike. I didn't know how it all worked, but it sounded pretty lousy for them if you ask me.

He said he wished he could be there to shout like hell for us because we'd need all the support we could get.

I was quite excited to try out our plan. We had nothing to lose, so we could only do normally or well. Even if we lost six–nil, it wouldn't look too bad.

My heart was really kicking as we got dressed that afternoon, as if something big was bound to happen, even though inside myself I could see us crumbling up front and all charging off to help the defenders.

We piled into the minibus and Mally stuck his elbow out on purpose as I slid onto the seat next to him, but I just ignored it. He couldn't injure me that easily, if that was what he was hoping to do. As we drove down to the field, everyone started singing a stupid beef burger song from a TV advert, and without realising it, I was singing along, much to Mally's disgust. He stared at me, all cheesed off, with his mouth glued shut. So I sang even louder.

Down at the field the Uplands team was already waiting for us, booting the ball to each other in their bright red-and-black, professional-looking soccer strip while we bundled out of the bus in our usual tattered selection of faded blue tops. You could almost see them laughing as they thought, "Not *them* again!"

I looked for Johannes to do a quick hand-rub, which had become our secret good luck signal, then remembered. The place seemed pretty empty without him sitting there. I wondered what was happening at Crossroads at that very moment, but then the whistle blew to call the captains and get the game ready, and there was no more time to think about him.

They won the toss and chose to play away from the road, so we were to kick off. As we got ready, Trevor nudged me and said, "It's not the same left back any more."

My heart did a sidestep. I'd forgotten about the useless back that was supposed to be against me. Downfield in front of me, instead of the lump of jelly I'd imagined, stood a sleek athlete with spiky blond hair, flexing and flicking his legs to loosen up, like a real pro. It was all I needed. Johannes not watching, and a World Cup soccer star marking my position.

We lined up. Andy put the ball on the centre spot and moved aside to let Trevor take the kick. There was a stiff silence as we waited for the whistle. Trevor gave me sort of a secret look as if to say, "Get ready, it's coming your way!"

My heart pounded.

The whistle scree'd.

Immediately voices started shouting, "Mark him, mark that ou," and calling for the ball. I ran down the line. Trevor tapped the ball to Andy, who returned it to him, then he turned to me for the long pass. But it never happened. The Uplands forwards charged down on him, and as he kicked, the ball thumped off one of them, surging into our own half, taking our defenders by surprise. Zak chased the ball, trapping it before it went out, but as he turned, the Uplands players were upon him. He struggled to keep possession, but they broke away with the ball, crossed it to their centre forward who controlled it with one foot, then shot effortlessly past Maurice for a goal.

It was hopeless. We were stunned. The game was all of thirty seconds old and we were already losing.

"Come on now, ous, *concentrate!*" Richard urged, clapping his hands together for emphasis. I was glad not to have to be captain at a time like that. It must have taken a lot to say anything to the team when they'd made such a mess of things.

I wished we could have called it a false start and kicked off again. The other team were actually laughing a bit, and chirping about trying to get hat tricks and things. So they thought they were really going to have us on toast. I looked hard at the blond bloke in front of me and decided that he wasn't going to scare me.

The whistle went again. Trevor shouted, "PIG!" and booted the ball upfield ahead of me, first touch, without giving them time to charge him down. It bounced towards the touch line and old blond spiky-head chased towards it. I sprinted after it, just keeping it in play and managing to steer past him without too much trouble. He chased after me, but I noticed that he couldn't catch me up. So he wasn't all that formidable after all.

Two other defenders closed in on me as I neared their corner line, and I was vaguely aware of Trevor, Andy and Richard shouting like mad for the ball in the centre. Without looking up, I chopped the ball a neat, lofted shot into the centre, where Andy and two of their blokes tackled for it. One of them cleared with a long kick downfield and into touch for our first throw-in.

It hadn't been a bad move. I noticed that we'd actually rattled them a bit, even if we didn't get that near to scoring.

Their defenders were all blaming each other for not taking me on. It's a wonderful feeling when you get the other team to start squabbling amongst themselves.

Trevor looked at me with a grin and gave a thumbs up. "Yeah, Pig, that's it! Just keep it on the ground next time. We'll get them."

One of their players overheard him and jeered, "Hah! hah!" at us, as if we'd never get another chance.

Trevor shook a fist at him and said, "You just wait and see."

I buzzed with adrenaline as we ran back, following the action into our half. Things were starting to cook. This time our defenders were awake and the going wasn't so easy for them. Alexander tackled someone twice his size and cleared up the wing to Benjy, and we all cheered and jeered at them at the same time, saying things like, "What's wrong with you ous? You can't even beat our tiniest player!" We weren't going to be the walkover they'd expected.

"Shut up!" they snapped, and worse things were said once the ref was out of earshot. The atmosphere was turning quite vicious as they swore at us and we cursed them back.

As long as Richard ran back and helped in defence when they came forward, the game was almost evenly matched, although I must say there were a few last gasp escapes and an amazing save by Maurice at our end that helped keep the score down to one goal.

Towards the end of the half I got another break down the wing and crossed a perfect shot on the ground right to Trevor's feet, but he lost it.

"Sorry," he called out, which was the first time any of them had ever said anything like that to me. It didn't mean much at the time though, because I was so wound up by the game.

Benjy and Trevor had a few chances to score, but the other team's keeper was a pretty hot shot and pulled off a couple of steaming saves.

Then a few minutes from half time they got another one.

Their centre forward broke past our defence and ran half the field on his own, easily beating Maurice.

During the break Mr Laing reckoned we were doing okay, but we were bunching too much. But then that was what he always said. Mally asked him if he could come on in my place, but he was told we were doing too well to interfere with the line-up as it was. I felt really good, but didn't let it show because, funnily enough, I actually pitied him a bit. I knew what it was like to have to sit and watch a game when all you wanted to do was get out there and play.

It was a pity Johannes wasn't there because I reckon he would have been proud of the way we'd played so far.

"Okay ous, we can still score," Richard reckoned. "Let's take the game to them!"

"Yeah!" we shouted. It was like an army getting all wound up for a battle.

We were on the attack again soon after the restart, with Trevor nearly scoring from Benjy's corner kick, but the shot went wide. The way we were playing, the goal had to come sooner or later. We couldn't come so close so many times without getting one. And it did. Exactly the way we'd planned it too. Francis played a long ball to me, I took it down the wing and clipped a quick cross to Trevor, who just blasted it past their keeper at point blank range.

We'd done it. We'd scored against Uplands! No one could believe it. Not them, nor us. The whistle blew and we screamed and leapt about like mad things. And they stared at us with daggers in their eyes and moped back to the halfway line, mumbling things we couldn't quite hear.

"Okay ous, one more, that's all we need!" Richard was really on form, clapping his hands together like slave whips to spur us on.

The game raged on, with them taking play into our half most of the time, but Francis, Zak and Leon threw everything they could at them to keep the shots out, and George Fergadiotis actually headed the ball off the line once, saving a definite goal when Maurice was well beaten. Of course all the Uplands blokes moaned that George was behind the line and it was already in and things, but they were just trying to crook, that's all.

We must have been in injury time with the score still at one-two, which we were more than pleased with, when Benjy broke away down the left wing for what had to be our last chance. Trevor, Andy and I screamed down the centre, yelling like crazy. Benjy crossed to Andy, who managed to dribble past two players, then slid a real pro pass to Trevor on the edge of the big box. I raced alongside him, hoping for a chance when he fired another powerful shot. In a reflex save, the goalie clapped the ball away with open hands, letting it fall at my feet as I charged down. There were frantic screams from all over the field as I took the shot. Then groans of agony as the ball sliced sideways against the post and shot back into play.

There was a sudden hush. As if everyone had stopped breathing. The world seemed to change into slow motion as the ball bounced across the goalmouth towards Trevor. The goalie scrambled after it, like someone crawling on the moon.

Trevor darted in with huge steps. One, two three . . . shut his eyes and kicked as the keeper lunged at his feet. The ball sped past his splayed hands, beneath his diving body, grazing a desperate defender and into the open goal.

The whistle blew at once for the goal and full time.

"Offside!" they shouted vainly.

We absolutely exploded. There's no other word for it.

"We drew with Uplands!" went the screams, the shouts, the roars and the whistles.

Trevor slapped my hand like those stupid volleyball players do, but it felt so good, I did it right back to him and we whooped together.

"Thanks for the game," we shouted at the Uplands players, but they just mumbled about how lucky we were.

Then most of them left with their stinking rich moms, calling "not fair" and "cheats" over their shoulders, which only made us feel better.

Five of them went off kicking sods of grass out of the pitch as they waited for their lifts to arrive, while our blokes sneaked into the clubhouse to change and shower. We weren't actually allowed to use the clubhouse, because we weren't proper members. We only had permission to use the second field because the school grounds were too small, but the blokes used to slip in as soon as Mr Laing had left. I suppose it made them feel like real main ou players, taking a shower in the clubhouse after a match. Especially after a good one like that.

"Coming for a shower, Pig?" Andy asked, which pretty much took me by surprise.

"Nah." Feelings towards me were clearly getting better, but somehow it didn't seem to matter any more. I'd had plenty of time to myself to think about things, and I'd decided that good friends like Phocho didn't come that easily after all. "I'm off to see a mate of mine," I lied.

I half expected him to get a dig at me for being chicken, but he didn't. Instead he said, "Well played, mun! Hell, we only got them a nice one, eh?"

"Yeah," I laughed.

"Okay, Pig, see you then."

"Yeah, cheers."

Sitting on the steps of the clubhouse, I unfolded the latest map of my life. It was actually quite odd how the roads had taken all sorts of turns and things that I'd never expected. Now that the huge mountains that had once stood in my way were gone, I no longer wanted to get beyond them. Others were there all right, but they were ones that looked as if they'd stay. Like what would the blokes have said if they ever found out that my best friend in the whole of Cape Town was an old Xhosa man? Peter was a mountain that could be crossed. He came along. He never called Johannes a boy again. And Francis was always okay inside. Just as long as the gang wasn't watching, that's all. Maybe even Trevor and the gang were crossable mountains. Maybe. I didn't reckon there was enough time to find that out, what with high school just around the corner, and us all going in different directions at the end of the year.

I wanted to head off over the fields towards home, but the five Uplands blokes were hanging around the river near Johannes's shack, mucking about, throwing stones and things, so I waited for them to move on. But they stayed in the same spot, throwing, and I got a bit impatient because our blokes would be out of the showers soon and see me still sitting outside. Then they'd think I had been too chicken to go in with them.

A stone hit the shack with a loud "dunk!" Then another did. They were aiming at it on purpose.

"No!" I shouted, but they didn't seem to hear me.

Something bad was happening. It wasn't just idle target practice, it was a gang of Whiteys attacking a helpless black man's house.

The sickness happened inside me again. The sickness I felt when Johannes told me about the riots and fighting in the townships that we never saw. Stuff we never knew about because we were kept away from it all on our side of town.

More stones hit, and then there were cheers as a little window pane shattered. It shattered inside me. I leapt from the steps and charged off across the field, shouting "Stop it! Leave him alone!" It was as if Johannes lay crumpled inside. As if he was in trouble at Crossroads right then.

One of them turned around and frowned into the sun at me coming, shook his head as if I was mad or something, and carried on throwing.

"Stop throwing stones. Who do you think you are?" I yelled, getting closer. "Get the hell out of here!"

"What?" One of them said.

"Get off this ground. It's private property."

"What's your hassle? It's only a kaffir hut."

Another pane smashed my voice into a scream: "GET OFF!" They stopped in surprise.

"Says who?" the biggest one challenged.

"I do."

"Oh yeah?"

Then one of them threw another stone. Quite a big rock that thudded against the flimsy door, rattling the bolts, stripping my self-control.

"I . . . said . . .", running at him in a blind fury, "STOP IT!"

My hands clawed round his wrists, nails digging in, and I shoved him over the river bank with my knee.

"Hey, little boy," one of them said menacingly, "you mean business, eh?"

Another one viced an arm round my neck from behind, choking my breath off and blurring my eyes. My elbows flew back, beating his ribs, trying to escape, but he only tightened his grip. I was Johannes at Crossroads. Two shapes came at me from the front. I kicked out hard, my foot cracking on something solid, and one of them crumpled and backed away. Then a fist sledge-hammered into my guts, sapping me into a pillow of weakness with one shot. A foot or something clapped ringing against the side of my head. Then the ground raced up and hit me in the face. Through one eye all I could see was a blur of grass, an inch away, and above the ringing there were distant voices shouting, "Rumble! Rumble! Come on ous, there's a rumble!"

Pounding kicks stoved at my ribs and crashed my head. I covered it with my arms, and studs grazed at my fingers, kicking my hands away. They cut and stamped into my legs too, but I hardly noticed because I couldn't breathe, and my rib cage ripped at me as they booted and punched. I wasn't even fighting back, but they kept on going. My nose flattened sideways on the ground, I couldn't see, and my teeth dug the mud as my mouth gaped for chokes of air.

"Rumble!" came the voices again above the ringing, and this time I recognised one of them. It was Trevor, yelling: "Get off, you bastards! Leave our friend. You bloody cowards, ten against one. Bugger off or we'll kill you!"

Leave our friend?!

The kicking and beating stopped, but I could still hear it.

Scuffling, shouts and punching somewhere else. I lifted my head. And there Trevor was, swinging wildly with both fists. He caught the biggest of them on the cheek and sent him toppling like a felled pine. Andy and Benjy caught him and got stuck in, then Trevor turned to see who was next. Richard crashed to the ground right next to me, pulling a bloke down on top of himself. Immediately Leon dived into the fray, while behind me Francis had someone screaming "Leave me, leave me! I didn't start it!"

"Yeah, well don't you kick an ou while he's down, (chop) you understand (chop)?"

"Yes!"

(Chop!) "Are you sure (chop) eh?"

"Yes!" came a frantic voice.

They got up and retreated sort of backwards, like hyenas, shouting things all the way, not daring to turn their backs on our blokes in case they attacked again.

Trevor came over and gave me a hand up. I winced as the porcupines shot pain all over me.

"Are you okay, Mike?" he asked, his brow furrowed.

Mike. Another first.

My head pounded and rang. I'd lost a horrible fight. But I'd just won one hell of a battle. The only thing was, it was a battle I'd long since lost any interest in trying to win.

Looking back

I suppose you could say things went a bit smoother after that day. Trevor stopped being such a bastard, and the others were pretty reasonable. (Only Mally never forgave me for taking his place in the team.) But I reckon life never gets any easier.

All I should say is, I managed.

Johannes stayed a secret, just like Peter's piano lessons did. Sort of compulsory to survival, I'm sorry to say.

I see quite a lot of Francis and Peter these days because we're at the same high school — quite a larney one in Newlands, actually — and now we're all fairly good connections. There's a stack more decent blokes in my class now, and I'm getting on pretty well with them. They actually see me as the sort of class comic because of the comments I chirp up with every now and again. Sometimes it gets me into a bit of trouble, but it's always worth it.

No one calls me Pig any more. Quite funny, really, I think I sort of miss it in a way!

I've hardly seen any of the others at all though, because we moved away from Wynberg just before the end of the year. I spotted Trevor from a bus once and we waved at each other. I heard he and Andy went to a real hooligan-type technical school where most of the blokes leave after Standard Eight.

Jenny's at a new school too, a much bigger one. I suppose she must be getting used to moving every five minutes. She's back onto Kit Kats again, and still manages to hold me to ransom for the odd one when she catches me up to something.

And Mom's met some bloke that we don't like too much. We try to get on with him most of the time, but secretly we hope they'll break it off, which is pretty lousy of us. We always get hopeful when she doesn't see him for a while. I don't reckon she'll actually marry him, I'm not quite sure why, but it's just a feeling I've got. Actually, to tell the truth, I think it's because she knows we can't stand him. Kids can be real brats sometimes, can't they?

Phocho and I still write regularly. He reckons he often remembers the good old days. Says they're long gone now. A company runs the farm, and the pigs are gone. Most of the sties lie empty and the others are being used for storage. He reckons that things have got really bad there recently. Lots of trouble in the compound and around Greytown in general: fighting, shooting, arrests . . . He says he'll have to join the struggle as soon as he's old enough. Sounds really horrible.

I just hope there'll be peace before it comes to that.

I took the bus to see how old Johannes was getting on a while ago. Took some more of Dad's old clothes for him. Only this time I asked Mom if I could first! But when I got to the fields, the old shack was gone. All that was left were the two stones we used to sit on, and the black patch from where the fire used to be.

I sat on my old rock for a while and then left the clothes there. Thought someone might want them.